The Wild Side Trilogy

MAGIC
—IN THE—
BLOOD

AF100601

MAGIC IN THE BLOOD

The Wild Side Trilogy

Michael Foster

Magic in the Blood

Copyright © 2025 Michael Foster

All rights reserved. No part of this publication may be reproduced, stored in any retrieval system, or transmitted in any form or by any means, mechanical, photocopying, recording, or otherwise, without permission in writing from the publisher, except by a reviewer, who may quote brief passages in a review.

This is a work of fiction. All of the characters, organizations, and events portrayed in this novel are either products of the author's imagination or are used fictitiously.

Cover and Interior design by Ted Ruybal
Interior illustrations by Gloria Miller Allen

Manufactured in the United States of America

Wisdom House Books
For more information, please contact:
www.wisdomhousebooks.com

Paperback ISBN: 979-8-9926345-0-1
Ebook ISBN: 979-8-9926345-1-8
LCCN: 2025907899

YAF019000 | YOUNG ADULT FICTION / Fantasy / General
YAF001000 | YOUNG ADULT FICTION / Action & Adventure / General
YAF062000 | YOUNG ADULT FICTION / Thrillers & Suspense / General

2 3 4 5 6 7 8 9 10
Second Edition 2025

DEDICATION

This book is dedicated to my mother, Alice.
She lived a life of unmatched kindness,
always choosing love over hate.

And to my daughter, Sabrina.
The magic of your blood flows strong
in here too.

And finally, to the entire community
of family and friends in Warm Lake.
You all inspired and helped shape this story.

TABLE OF CONTENTS

Prologue ix
1. Everything Old and New 1
2. Pancakes, Preparations, & Promises 21
3. Changes 33
4. Voices on a Mountain Trail 41
5. A Gruesome Discovery 49
6. The Burning Girl 57
7. Arguments & Understandings 69
8. A Meeting with Destiny. 81
9. Truth & Lies 93
10. Sorrow 99
11. Wisdom from Bob 109
12. Jellies of the Lake. 119
13. The Rumbling Slumberer 127
14. Gigantic Proportions. 141
15. All is (Temporarily) Right. 153
16. A Softly Simmering Anger 161
17. A Clash of Titans. 169
18. Lost Love 177
19. Somewhere, a Legend Dies 185
20. What Matters the Most 199
Afterward. 205
About the Author 209

"One's anger is one's greatest enemy and one's calmness is one's protection."

—Sathya Sai Baba—

"Return to the land of your fathers; blood calls to blood."

—Horton Deakins—

PROLOGUE

A light wind caressed the tips of the long grass, as the porcupine meandered through low brush at the edge of the large clearing. Pausing for a moment, he looked across the wide space, squinting in the early morning light. The porcupine's eyesight was terrible, but his sensitive nose was invaded by a myriad of pleasing scents drifting on the breeze that tousled his short fur. Smells of sage and wildflower floated by, and he was happy as he continued his search for breakfast.

 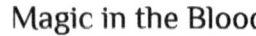 

A late summer rainstorm had recently come through. The downpour brought the chubby creature out from the woods that surrounded the clearing, searching for tender growths he knew would have freshly sprouted from the wet earth. The porcupine was accustomed to eating wood, bark, and stems, his typical diet, and he would often sneak into campgrounds at night to chew on boat paddles, an unwelcome surprise for boaters to wake up to. An excellent climber as well, stealing fruit left out on messy picnic tables by careless campers was no challenge at all, as long as the bears hadn't gotten to the goodies first. For the moment, however, he was looking for young plant buds pushing up through the moist soil. These were special treats he knew he would find after a good rain.

Discovering a small patch of new shoots, the scruffy creature settled in to nibble at the green stalks, eyes darting left and right, always wary of predators. The porcupine was, by nature, a slow-moving creature, but in reality, he had little fear of most animals. His thousands of quills were a natural defense, and if any of the denizens of the forest came too close, he would simply raise the needle-like projections which normally laid flat across his back. With quills erect, he could almost be mistaken for a large pincushion, furry, yet undeniably dangerous. A quick whip of his tail could embed several of the quills into the face or paw of any attacker, sending them howling in pain. It is a sorrowful lesson many curious dogs have learned.

The porcupine happily feasted on young grass buds as the sun warmed his fur, still damp from the rainstorm. Suddenly, he felt a sharp stab in his foot. A pain in his small front paw, like stepping on a huge thistle thorn. Quickly, he tugged his paw back, but it

 **Prologue**

wouldn't move from the spot. Bracing his other feet against the ground, he jerked the trapped leg, tugging repeatedly to pull his foot away from moist soil, his meal now forgotten. The efforts were fruitless, the porcupine's paw was firmly stuck!

Eyes wide with pain and nose twitching frantically, the quilled creature looked closely at his paw and saw what appeared to be a stick poking up right through his foot. As he stared, the pointy object, pale and translucent as a bean sprout, began to stretch, longer and longer, rising like a snake before him. The frightened porcupine struggled harder now, making a series of grunts and whines. He gaped as the frightening growth pulsed and flexed, bending to the side, like a soggy french fry, the tip curving slowly back toward the ground. The pointy blood-specked tip drove down into the ground, pulling hard and trapping the creature's paw tightly against the earth.

Desperation raced through the porcupine's small brain as he began violently thrashing, trying to free himself. He pushed against the ground with all four feet, tugging and finally trying to chew through this stick that held him in place. A second pale stick burst explosively through the dirt next to his other front paw, whipping out and curling around the small leg quick as lightning.

The porcupine reacted defensively in the only way he knew how, raising his quills and lashing his tail back and forth, attacking the air around him in search of a target. He was used to danger from above or around him, never from below, and sadly his protective efforts were wasted. He had no idea how to face and deter this enemy.

Rain-soaked dirt sprayed into the air as more of the translucent sticks pierced upwards from the soil like small daggers of varying thickness, some as slender as spaghetti, some as fat as a pencil.

Slowly, yet unavoidably, they began wrapping themselves around the porcupine, sliding like bleached worms through his fur, feeling their way between the raised quills that posed no threat. The sticks flexed and tightened like rubber bands or bungee cords, pulling him flat against the soil until he could no longer move at all.

The porcupine's terrified, high-pitched screams chased the soft breeze across the wide meadow of wildflowers, which bent the petals with its scented passing. The creature struggled to breathe as he was inescapably covered by the mass of pulsing and deadly worm-things. At last, his horrified cries were silenced by an all-encompassing blanket of wood that encased his trembling body.

All that remained visible to any random hiker or wild animal that may pass by was a small, rounded mound of sticks woven together like an overturned wicker basket. It was unusual in appearance, yes. It might even be considered odd enough to spark interest in someone and perhaps a closer, curious inspection.

However, a casual glance would not tell the whole story. For inside that overturned wicker basket, there in the suffocating darkness, small white roots, like thick needles, slowly extended upward into the soft belly of the creature trapped within.

Gran'Tree, the great yellow pine, tasted the blood of the porcupine and sighed in pleasure. He spread further beyond the boundaries of the meadow, the vast network of his shriveled roots quickly expanding once again.

And he fed.

1

EVERYTHING OLD AND NEW

The autumn morning was cool, the sun only recently risen, not yet providing enough heat to chase away the heavy chill of night. The slowly brightening forest was hushed, as if all who inhabited it were treating it with the reverence of an abandoned church, communicating only in whispers for fear of disturbing any remaining deity or ghosts that had chosen to set up permanent residence. The quiet was broken only by the distant call of birds, passing through on their migratory path south, and the occasional loud "clik."

Alicia stood on the front porch of her log cabin, absentmindedly snapping the thumb and middle finger of her right hand together. *Clik!* Fire blossomed in her hand, flickering bright and orange. The young girl let it burn, watching the fire nestle there, snuggling into her palm like a tiny kitten. If she raised her hand to her ear and listened, she could hear a faint crackling sound. After a few moments, she shook her hand and extinguished the small flame, then repeated the process again.

The log cabin was Alicia's family's summer vacation home, set in the woods of central Idaho. A seasonal getaway from city life, where they could all enjoy a bit of freedom from the stresses back home. *The great outdoors*, Alicia thought, the sarcasm invading her mind driven by a recollection of her recent adventures in the Wild Side.

The single-room building was built from real pine logs and was, by any definition, rustic. It had beds at one end, a queen for her parents and a bunk bed for Alicia, pushed against opposite walls.

 # Everything Old and New

There was a small table for dining and a kitchenette just big enough to cook small meals for Alicia and her parents. The bunk bed had been purchased with the idea of a larger family in mind, but for now, Alicia was an only child.

A large, wood-burning stove, heavy and dark, stood in the corner near the front door. At night, Alicia could barely make out its shadow and imagined it to be a huge beast guarding the entrance from dangerous forest intruders, whatever they might be.

The stove had a large door in the front center that opened to expose an oven which was occasionally used for baking. Alicia loved when her family baked. They made a project of it, with her father, mother, and herself each filling different roles. Her mother measured out the dry goods, Alicia got to crack the eggs into the mix and add other wet ingredients. Her father would blend it all together, his arm working tirelessly with the whisk, finally putting the baking tray in the oven, which, Alicia knew, would soon fill the cabin with the wonderful scents of fresh bread or cookies.

The cabin was built by her grandfather long before Alicia was born. While adventuring as a young man, his travels brought him into a small narrow valley where he discovered the most beautiful lake, not too big or too small. It was perfect for boating, fishing, and simply enjoying the outdoors.

The cool mountain air was fresh and clean. For some people, "fresh and clean" could mean the smell of a city after a thunderstorm when the asphalt warmed and released a sharp tang into the air. For others, it meant the salty, briny smell of the beach when the sea breeze carried the heavy and pungent odor of seafood on the verge of going bad. This was neither of those.

Everything Old and New

No, the air around the lake carried a hint of pine and earth, but not the fake chemical pine that drifts through so many cars, seeping from little green cardboard trees hanging from rearview mirrors. Instead, this was the smell of home, the morning after finding the perfect tree for Christmas and setting it up in the family room, but before the other holiday scents of cinnamon, nutmeg, and cloves have had a chance to claim their hold.

Alicia's grandfather knew he wanted to spend as much time as possible in this forested hidden valley. With a few hired hands, he built a perfect little cabin, complete with a covered front porch. From his chair there on the wooden porch, her grandfather could sit in the mornings with the newly wakened birds and watch the sunrise over the mountains, steam rising off the lake's water, so still, it reflected the land and sky as perfectly as any mirror. And in the evenings, he could stuff his pipe full of pungent tobacco and see the moon, full and bright, climb above the hills and stir the owls to call out with a loud "Hoo, hoo!"

In the years to follow, many more families found their way to this little slice of heaven and built cabins of their own around the peaceful lake. They created a wonderful, thriving community of friends that, in many ways, felt like one big family.

Alicia was fourteen years old now. Her grandfather left this world when she was very young, her grandmother following shortly after. Her only real memories of them were her grandfather's stern yet fair discipline and the hard, sugary lemon candies her grandmother always kept in a small porcelain dish. She would allow Alicia to have one, and only one, each day.

These days, it was Alicia's family that would escape to this summer spot in the woods as often as her parents' jobs would allow.

Alicia loved spending summers in this wilderness, so vastly different from her city life. She had been coming to the cabin since she was born and spent a lot of time growing up in these woods. Her parents gave Alicia the freedom to roam (within reason). They instilled a sense of confidence and trust in her own abilities, as well as helping her to develop her own sort of internal GPS. She understood the location of major landmarks and had never lost her way on the trails she loved to hike.

Here, Alicia explored the dense forest, swam in the cool lake while looking for small frogs and other wildlife, and read books like a starving man eats. It was her favorite place in the whole world. And it was always with a heavy heart that she packed away her summer clothes, her shorts and tank tops, bathing suits, and her worn hiking boots, into her red suitcase in preparation for a return to city life.

Now, things had changed. And the once familiar dark woods hid new secrets, some amazing and some that she had yet to fully understand.

Last night had been one of those extra chilly nights, where when exhaling, you see your breath hanging in the air, and every word spoken outdoors was accompanied by a small cloud of vapor. Alicia's father had kept the wood stove burning low all night, waking every few hours to crawl out of bed and sleepily stuff another chunk of wood onto the remaining coals. He would watch it catch fire and burn before closing the small metal door on the stove and returning to bed.

The cold clung to the woods this morning. It lingered in the shadowy spaces, held tightly to branches like dusty, abandoned spiderwebs in the rafters of an old barn despite the sun's valiant attempts to drag it away with fingers of crisp light that pushed aside the blue-green needles of the surrounding pine trees. Alicia's bare arms were dappled with tiny goosebumps, and when she inhaled, her mouth felt like she had been sucking on a peppermint, but she didn't pay much attention to the sensations. Instead, she focused, snapping her fingers once again to watch the warm flames gently dance.

Alicia's ears detected a soft rustling sound coming from the trees. Her eyes dragged slowly away from her fingers as if she had been hypnotized by the magic. She looked up and scanned the woods, searching for the source of the sound.

The world was brighter and more vividly colored than normal, as if some great magical being had soared swiftly through the forest, marking up everything in sight, like an over-excited child with their first highlighter pen. Alicia knew, in some ways, that wasn't far from the truth.

The destruction of the barrier which once stood between the land of humans and the magical realm of the Wild Side, destruction that Alicia herself caused just days before, had unleashed the magic of the Wild Side into her own world. Now the depths of the forest appeared to pop in high definition. Like that moment you rise from the water after a swim, wipe the moisture from your eyes and see your surroundings glittering with renewed clarity. The world just . . . didn't quite glow, exactly. But it was as if the rocks, the leaves—all that she could see had a thin border of light around their edges.

Everything was motionless. Not a single leaf or pine needle quivered in the still morning air. Alicia strained to hear, for a moment thinking the rustling sounds must have just been her imagination, focused as she had been on her magic. Stubby, dense bushes had turned yellow and orange with the coming Autumn, like old farm machinery left out to rust, and filled the spaces between the trees. Alicia squinted to see, waiting, listening.

As she watched, the thin leafy branches parted, and a huge paw emerged, followed by a lean face with narrowed eyes. The largest cougar she had ever seen stepped forward into the sun, golden in color, with prominent dark scars along its flank and massive paws that housed long, sharp claws.

Alicia's breath came quick at the sight of the fearsome cat. In an instant, her face broke into a huge toothy smile. Alicia shook out the flames dancing in her palm and leaped off the wooden porch. Falling to her knees, she reached out and beckoned to the cougar, which moved toward her, each step leaving a small impression in the dirt.

"Hi, Tawny!" she cried, throwing her arms around the thick neck of the huge cat, feeling the corded muscle beneath the fur. Tawny's hot breath tickled her ear, and she squeezed tighter. It had been a day and a half since she last saw the great beast. Alicia had begun to fear the cat chose to return to the Wild Side. *Well, the Wild Side is everywhere now, isn't it? Thanks to me,* she mused. *The whole world is just one big, wild, magical realm!*

Alicia was an intelligent, adventurous girl, and up until a few weeks ago, she had been just like any other girl her age, preparing

to enter high school, filled with equal parts excitement and anxiety over how her life would change. Would she make new friends? Would she enjoy her classes? Would she start a relationship? But so much happened in the past few weeks. Her life HAD changed, no doubt about it! And she had no idea what the future held for her or her family.

Three years ago, when Alicia was just eleven, she became separated from her father in the woods. She had noticed an unusual disturbance in the air and went to investigate, stepping through an invisible barrier between her realm and the Wild Side, discovering a parallel world of magic ravaged by a terrible event called The Drying.

An enormous tree named Gran'Tree had stretched its roots throughout that realm and was drinking up all the water in the land, bringing death to the many animals and other more magical creatures that lived there.

Alicia discovered some unexpected new friends in the Wild Side. Mickey, a squirrel who was always hungry, was the first to greet her as she stepped into the new world and was there to support her as she grieved the absence of her family. Briar, the noisy jay who enjoyed sneaking food (*part of the reason Mickey was always hungry*), joined them soon after. Fiona, the gentle deer who couldn't speak words, communicated by sending thoughts and images into Alicia's head becoming a surrogate mother of sorts to the band of travelers. There was also the terrifying, yet surprisingly kind mountain troll, Bristleback, who brought the troop to their ultimate goal but lost his life to The Drying, returning to the sand and dust from which he was created.

Together, the five travelers journeyed south to the valley of

Gran'Tree, the source of The Drying, and there, Alicia confronted the great tree and discovered a way to return home, back through the barrier.

She had been surprised that even though her journey had taken her several weeks, she learned that only fifteen minutes had passed back home. When Alicia told her father, sick with worry for those few minutes, he didn't believe a word of her story, and her mother had been angry with her after learning of her "wandering off."

And now, the barrier was down. The hidden barrier that separated Alicia's mundane . . . *No wait, that's not fair*, she admitted to herself. Her world was far from mundane. It was just . . . normal . . . compared to that side—the magical world of the Wild Side with its sprites, trolls, ancient beings, and talking animals!

The barrier had been in place for hundreds of years, thousands if you look at it from the viewpoint of the denizens of the Wild Side, where time used to flow at a different speed. With the barrier now gone, she imagined that time moved at the same speed across both realms, hers and theirs.

Alicia had been tricked by the great yellow pine, Gran'Tree, but she didn't know for what reason. She had thought she was done with the Wild Side and had even begun to think that her parents had been right. Maybe it had all been her imagination. Three years had passed since that crossing in the rain, and she no longer felt the magic.

But then one day, just a few short weeks ago, Alicia stepped from the cabin to find her parents frozen in the woods, trapped and motionless within an unbreakable, transparent bubble. Alicia immediately recognized the bubble as magical and understood

with absolute certainty that not only had she been right about the existence of the Wild Side, but that she would have to return there seeking help.

The determined teen found her way to Gran'Tree once again and talking with him, was fooled into believing the tree was being kind and had been trying to help her. In the end, it was her own fault that she'd smashed the barrier, but she was only trying to save her parents. Save them from a danger that *she* might have inadvertently caused by crossing the barrier in the first place.

Gran'Tree had known what would happen when she destroyed the frozen bubble of time that trapped her mom and dad. He knew and kept that information to himself—a secret from Alicia. *Would I have made the same decision to save my parents, knowing what would happen? Well, of course I would! But Gran'Tree still lied to me. Lied by omission anyway, which is almost as bad.*

Her parents, Richard and Kate, had not been aware of anything happening during Alicia's search for help on the Wild Side. How could they? They were frozen in time. Time that was leaking into her "ordinary" realm through cracks in the barrier, disrupting the flow of her world. But her mom and dad knew now.

She had told them stories about visiting the Ancients. Thunderbolt was one of them, a being who controlled the power of storms. He had climbed the tallest peak around the lake to live out his days in a small, rundown shack, constantly reaching for the sky to regain power. All that stretching actually lengthened his body, making him taller than any human she had ever seen before.

Then there was Vulcan. She lived near a large, natural hot spring deep within the forest, which filled the nearby woods with drifting clouds of steam and the scent of sulfur, which smelled a bit like old eggs. She had the power of fire at her fingertips, like Alicia herself, and controlled the sprites. Those tiny flying beings could light up the dark like fireflies, with colorful glowing displays that shone from their bodies. They sent visions of what they saw to the Ancient. The steam and heat of the hot springs had, over several millennia, washed away any details from Vulcan's skin, leaving behind a creature of unnatural, yet unmatched beauty. A living being appearing carved from marble, featureless, shining white and glorious.

In her final encounter, Alicia had gone deep underground into the old, dank, abandoned mines leftover from a time long ago when humankind still co-existed with the citizens of the Wild Side. She went to seek an audience with The Silver King, a horrid creature. His body was bloated and waterlogged, decaying from years of living in the wet dark, slowly turning into the mud that surrounded him. She thought he could help with his powers of earth. At first it seemed he would, but she fled his terrible domain in terror when she realized that this Ancient only wanted to drain the power he saw within her, claiming it for himself so that he could rise again.

Long ago, the Ancients came together in a valley far to the south. There, the Ancients used their combined magic to create the barrier, forever dividing the world of magic from the world of humans. In doing so, they not only drained most of their own magical powers, but they also transferred some of that power to a seedling, unnoticed at the time, which had now become a giant, sentient yellow pine.

Failing to find help from the Ancients, Alicia had to resort to meeting with that very yellow pine, Gran'Tree. The same great

 ## Everything Old and New

pine she had convinced to stop his plundering and damaging ways during her first visit to his world. There, she rediscovered her power. A power she thought was lost, or maybe just imagined in the make-believe days of her childhood. A power she used to help free her mother and father from the bubble of time and, in the process, completely shatter the barrier between worlds.

Alicia's magic was back and manifesting in new and exciting ways! She couldn't imagine what the full extent of her power might be and was eager to discover it.

Alicia gave the massive cat one more scratch on her furry head, stood, and looked into the forest once more. Everything felt more . . . *alive* than it had since the barrier had come down. She could almost see movement in the soil as insects crawled beneath its surface, through the rich earth and mulch. If she watched long enough, Alicia imagined she would see tree limbs bend toward one another as hushed and private conversations took place through the brush of pine needles, sounding like the singing of crickets' legs. This must have been what her grandfather experienced when he first discovered this place, long before the region became populated with vehicles and the air was filled with the sounds of human presence.

The forest's deep greens, fiery oranges, and rich browns shone like the bright, waxy color of crayons, as if she had stepped into Oz from a black-and-white landscape. Or even Wonka's famous chocolate factory. She could hear bird song, squirrel chatter, and maybe even words in those voices that she hadn't heard in a very long time. Magic had returned to her world! Alicia raised her hand, snapping her fingers again, watching in amazement as the flames cavorted across her fingertips. She felt . . . powerful!

The cabin door opened behind her with a quiet squeak of rusty hinges as Alicia's father came out onto the porch, feeling the shock of stepping from the warm interior into the cool morning air, rubbing his arms vigorously as he attempted to banish the goosebumps forming there. "Whatcha doin', kiddo?"

Alicia glanced back at her father. Richard was a strong man of average height who fancied himself a lumberjack. Back home, he wore a nice suit to work, but out here, it was jeans and flannel shirts most of the time. Sure, he could cut down a few dead trees for firewood during the summers, but her dad wasn't out climbing trees with a rope and harness. And he did not wear the obligatory outdoorsman's beard either.

Alicia saw her father's attention was drawn to the brightness resting gently in her upturned hand. She quickly shook her fingers, extinguishing the flames, as if she had been caught carrying out something she shouldn't have been doing.

"Nothing," she quickly replied, resentful that he'd intruded on her moment. Alicia sensed that her father, a kind and normally supportive person, feared this new and surprising magic. Or, at the very least, he disapproved of what he saw. It made sense, of course. After all, seeing your daughter's fingers on fire would scare any parent. Or anybody else for that matter. Still, she was annoyed at his apparent lack of acceptance.

Something else that terrified both of her parents was the presence of Tawny. Her mom and dad made a point to keep their distance from the cougar, and now her father watched Tawny. Alicia saw an expression of distrust sliding across his face, replacing the look of disapproval at the use of her own magic. The large cat

seemed to sense his discomfort as well and took a few steps back to indicate she was not a threat to him or his daughter.

The Ancient, Thunderbolt, sent the cougar to accompany Alicia on her previous journey. While she had initially been frightened of the beast, they eventually formed an unbreakable bond. She loved the cat with all her heart.

Her parents were trying to understand this bond, trying to allow their fears to fade. But accepting that their young daughter was friends with this wild and, let's face it, dangerous animal? That was too much. Alicia and Tawny's connection went against every sane, rational reality the couple knew, and they struggled hard with it, even though their daughter explained that the cat had saved her life.

"It's going to be a beautiful day, isn't it?" her father asked, awkwardly avoiding the issue at hand, trying to make small talk and pretending things were normal when they were *so* far from normal it wasn't funny. Now that the magic was back, Alicia didn't know what normal meant anymore.

"It is," she answered, playing along. "But the air feels colder than usual this morning. I wonder how many more clear days we'll have before it starts to rain again." She looked over her shoulder at her dad. "That thunderstorm the other night was really strong. We should leave soon," she said, bringing the conversation back to a difficult topic.

When Alicia spoke of leaving, she wasn't talking about going back home to the city where they spent winter. She and her parents had spoken a lot, arguing over the past few days about their next steps. Richard and Kate were ready to return home, but Alicia felt responsible for what had happened to the barrier between worlds.

She didn't know if any damage might result from taking it down. Alicia knew she had to convince her parents to let her go to the Wild Side and talk to Thunderbolt again. After all, he and the other Ancients had created the barrier in the first place. He must know what to do next and if there was any way to restore it. It was the only answer.

After several back-and-forth conversations, much hesitancy on the part of her parents, and more than a few angry exchanges, they eventually agreed to allow their determined daughter to make the trip, but only on one condition. There was absolutely no way they were letting her go alone. Even though she had explored the Wild Side independently twice and did very well for herself both times she told them, her father insisted on traveling with her this time. *Stupid*, she thought. But what could she do?

Richard's sigh let Alicia know that even though he had agreed to this trip, he was not looking forward to it. They normally enjoyed long summer hikes together, but she could see that now he was confused by this new reality. Determined, she had to prove to her parents, and to herself, by showing them.

"Well, if we're gonna do this," he said with another sigh, "let's get some breakfast in our bellies and then start packing. Your mom's mixing up huckleberry pancake batter, which I gotta get cooking. It should keep us nice and full for a while. We'll take trail mix and breakfast bars for tomorrow morning and grab some berries along the way."

The plan was to take the car to the hiking trail in the hills—no more trying to find her path on deer trails!—and to get close to the summit of Thunderbolt's mountain tonight. Alicia and her father would set up camp and finish the hike tomorrow morning, meet with Thunderbolt by early afternoon, and with any luck, be home by dark. That is, if he would see them at all. The Ancient seemed to be a bit of a recluse the first time Alicia met him. She hoped that the barrier coming down would make him more talkative this time.

Together, Alicia and her father would find the answers they needed. The answer *she* needed revolved around her magic; most importantly, could she use her powers to fix the barrier? Maybe the Ancients had rested long enough to restore their own power and would now be able to rebuild it themselves.

Or was the extraordinary destined to become ordinary? Would magic become commonplace? Would trolls and fairies enter her realm? Would more people, maybe even her friends, discover magic powers of their own? She hoped any damage she caused the world was not irreparable. But, if she was being honest with herself, Alicia wasn't holding much hope.

"Yeah, let's eat," Alicia replied. Heavy thoughts weighed on her, but a spark of excitement grew in her chest like the flames that bloomed in her hand. "I'm hungry!"

Waving goodbye to the dusty cat, she and her father stepped back into the warm embrace of the cabin.

A gathering of raccoons was heading home a short distance from the small cabin, prepared to settle down to sleep for the day. They were nocturnal creatures, exploring the woods at night to find tasty insects or maybe even scoop a fish from the edge of the lake if they got lucky. With the sunrise, they made their way home, in this case, a neighbor's tool shed with a rather large crawlspace below. One of the baseboards on the outside had come loose, creating a perfect entry point for the mischievous bandits.

Entering their den, the leader of the group paused, listening. His hyper-sensitive hearing could detect the sound of motion underneath the soil, like earthworms sliding through the dirt. The morning sun filtered down through gaps in the rickety shed's walls and floorboards, reflecting off fresh spiderwebs spun quickly during the night by their eight-legged owners. The dim sunlight lit the crawlspace with patches of dirty yellow glow.

The raccoon moved deeper into the den, his three companions following single-file behind, disturbing a web near the entrance and sending a particularly fat spider scurrying away. The raccoon would happily partake in one more snack before going to sleep, and a juicy worm would be perfect!

Following his ears, the raccoon moved to the middle of the dingy crawlspace and dug into the dirt, searching. His long fingers uncovered a white, pulsing strand, which moved like a worm, but didn't quite look or smell right. Like the back of a caterpillar walking along a tree branch, a section of the strand pushed upward as he watched. The raccoon hissed a warning, not liking what he was seeing.

The chittering group of friends behind the leader crowded close to discover what was so interesting. In doing so, they bumped him forward, and he involuntarily stepped into the small hole he had dug. His dirty paw brushed through and underneath the loop that had formed in the strand. In the blink of an eye, it tightened down fast.

The raccoon squealed and ripped his paw free, tumbling backwards

and causing the entire group to spring back. Loud chatter immediately filled the space as each member of the tribe ran to a separate corner, spinning back to stare at the long white thing that now whipped back and forth, seeking flesh.

The leader heard a new sound coming from below ground and felt a vibration in his paws. It was as if a thousand worms were all converging on one spot. And they were coming fast. An unfamiliar fear gripped him, and he made a move toward the exit. But it was too late.

The dirt floor of the crawlspace exploded upwards. A mass of white thrashing roots engulfed the dim space, each swinging wildly until it encountered a warm body, wrapping tightly around whatever appendage it happened to hit. Some of the roots pinned the creatures down, while others viciously stabbed into their soft bodies, sucking, drinking, draining them of blood.

The smallest raccoon of the clan, the newest addition and as such, the last to enter the crawlspace, was also the luckiest of the group. He was closest to the loose baseboard exit when the explosion of dirt came. He turned and immediately fled.

Stepping into daylight, confused but relieved, the littlest raccoon paused to look around and understand where to go. He was tensed and ready to bolt, furry haunches quivering, but he had followed his pack for so long, he felt lost without them. This space had been home since leaving his family. What was he to do?

Frantically, the little cub looked back and forth, his quick eyes tracking left and right in terror. Picking a random direction, he set out to find help. And he may have escaped if he had only been a little faster.

Before he could move, like paper streamers from a confetti cannon, several roots sprang from the ground around him. They smothered the small creature, squeezing and driving the breath from his lungs before he could squeak.

While behind him, the massacre in the crawlspace continued.

2
PANCAKES, PREPARATIONS, & PROMISES

Alicia bounced into the cabin, grinning, and plopped herself down into a chair at the table. She was more than ready to get this journey on the road, but at the moment Alicia was more excited about breakfast. The tense grumbled conversations of the past few days had taken away her appetite. Now that they had all settled on a plan, and she and her father were about to leave, she could hear the grumbles coming from her stomach instead. And huckleberry pancakes were her favorite! The sweet, tangy purple berries made everything better, especially pancakes. The familiar scent filling the cabin caused Alicia to salivate so much that she swallowed in anticipation, knowing this morning's batch would be better than ever.

Her father positioned himself at what he called the "Griddle of Goodness," really just a frying pan for cooking the pancakes. Kate brought the batter to where he stood armed with a can of spray oil, a spatula, and a bowl of huckleberries, ready to be added to the cakes as they cooked.

Alicia sat at the table watching this performance impatiently. The table was already set with colored plates and butter sitting on a dish, softened and shapeless from the cabin's heat. Alongside that stood a bottle of maple syrup, its handle slightly sticky with residue.

Her parents moved with coordination born from years together, Alicia's mother pouring a cupful of batter onto the sizzling pan, and her father plunking in berries one at a time before flipping the cake, moving the completed ones to a growing stack.

Pancakes, Preparations, & Promises

"Uuuughhh, come on!" Alicia said, holding a fork in one hand and a knife in the other like some ancient warrior at a medieval roast. "I'm starving!"

"Well maybe you should have thought of that last night when you chose to skip dinner," her mother said. She was not at all pleased with her daughter's behavior the past few days.

Alicia quieted down, but continued to eyeball the growing stack of pancakes, wondering how many she could stuff in her belly.

"Done," her father finally said as he turned off the griddle and placed the last pancake on the plate. "Let's eat!" Moving around the counter, he picked up the wobbly tower of cakes and carried them to the table.

"Thanks, Mom, thanks Dad," Alicia said loud enough to drown out the rumbles in her tummy, which were on the verge of growing painful. Excitedly, she reached for three pancakes before her father set the serving plate on the table and piled them onto her dish. Alicia lifted the hot cakes carefully with her fingers, one at a time, and used her knife to smear a thick pat of yellow butter on each, laying the next cake on top to melt the butter between. In her haste to get the syrup bottle, she almost knocked over her drinking glass, small and green, filled with fresh squeezed orange juice. Only a last-minute saving grab kept the liquid from spilling across the flowered vinyl tablecloth.

"Hey, hey. Slow down," her mother said. "The pancakes aren't going anywhere."

"Sorry," Alicia replied as she poured a generous helping of rich syrup in a swirling pattern across the stack of cakes. Inhaling the caramel-like scent, she watched the sticky liquid pour deliciously over the sides of the pancakes like tiny, golden waterfalls of amber sweetness that stretched into thin lines and combined with the butter melting from between the layers before dripping to create a shimmering pool around the base. She could almost see the reflection of her excitement in that buttery pool and dipped her finger in before sucking the syrup off. "Mmmm."

"Thank you, hon," Richard said to his wife, pulling a slightly wobbly chair out from the small kitchen table. "Alicia, use your fork, please." Sinking into the chair, he watched his daughter's enthusiasm, wishing he still had the metabolism of youth to splurge like that. Instead, he took a reasonable *two* pancakes, knowing he could have more if he was still hungry.

"It was a team effort," Kate said, grinning as she watched the two of them digging in. She reached out and stroked Alicia's hair briefly before turning back toward the kitchenette. Alicia looked up at the touch of her mom's fingers, watching her grab her favorite coffee cup, the one with the chipped rim and a faded cartoon drawing of a deer on the side, from where it sat near the warm stove. Kate topped it off with fresh coffee from the mostly empty pot before joining them at the table, taking two pancakes as well, smearing a small bit of butter on each. "You two are going to have quite an adventure," she said while pouring a reserved amount of syrup across her cakes, preferring the tangy sweetness of the huckleberries to the overpowering maple flavor.

Alicia paused with a mouthful of food and scowled at her mother. After days of arguing about it, she felt it was very unfair that her mother now seemed to be celebrating their trip. "I'm just glad you *finally* believe me," Alicia said, slowly drawing out the

Pancakes, Preparations, & Promises

word "finally" to show her indignation. "Remember, *you* thought I was just lost three years ago. I tried to tell you, but neither of you would listen. Said I made it all up."

Alicia saw her mom lift the coffee cup, her eyes looking over the rim at her dad as she sipped quietly. Alicia imagined the unspoken message passing between them. *Here we go again.*

And it was true. Today was probably the hundredth time Alicia had mentioned their lack of belief in her during the past week since saving her parents. She didn't feel they fully appreciated that fact. Of course, they had not exactly been aware they needed saving, being frozen in time and all that. *It's just nice to be proven right,* she thought, *and it would be even nicer if they could actually acknowledge it.*

Neither her mom nor dad had believed Alicia when she first told them about crossing over to the Wild Side three years ago, chalking the story up to her vivid imagination, which *was* quite vivid, given the number of books she read. This situation was just like a time she had been sitting by the window watching a brown bear wander through the woods not far from the cabin. Her mother said it was probably one of the neighboring cabin owners' dogs out exploring. Like Alicia didn't know the difference between a dog and a bear! She said as much to her mom. But Kate didn't believe Alicia, and her dad had taken her mother's side. So, Alicia had let it go, like so many other things, because children never win fights with adults. And over time, she had begun to doubt her own memories. Why was it that parents, and most grown-ups for that matter, have such a tough time believing kids?

Alicia was going to savor this victory, so she had no problem repeating herself as many times as she had to, to prove her point.

Each declaration gave her another sense of vindication.

"We believe *something* happened," her mom said, waving in the direction of the front porch. "I don't know how to explain that trick you do with your fingers or that beast wandering around outside." She reached for her coffee mug again. "But clearly, there is more going on than your father or I understand. Which is why we both agreed to this little hike." Alicia bristled at the dismissive tone in her mother's voice when she said, "little hike," and felt her shoulders tighten, prepared to argue again. "But your father and I also have work to get back to," her mother continued, "and *you* need to get prepared for high school. It's a big year for you. So, finish your breakfast, and you two can get a move on. The faster this nonsense is over, the better."

"Fine," Alicia said, her voice dark and deep with barely restrained anger. "I'm done eating anyway." She guzzled the rest of her orange juice, some slopping out of the glass and rolling down her cheeks. Alicia wiped her face quickly and pushed away her plate, leaving half of her stack uneaten, slowly becoming soggy with syrup. She stood up and headed off to start packing for the trip.

Finishing the last few bites of his own pancakes, Richard looked silently again at Kate as if to say, "Can't you let her have this one win?" He rose from the table, gathered his dish as well as Alicia's abandoned plate, scraping her leftovers into the garbage before washing the dishes and placing them to dry.

"Alright, kiddo, let's do this. Don't forget extra batteries for your flashlight. And roll your sleeping bag super tight. It will make it less bulky on your back for the hike."

"Ok, Dad." Alicia already knew this, even though she had not

Pancakes, Preparations, & Promises

taken a sleeping bag on her last trip. Being in such a panic, she had packed quickly, only taking a thin blanket that would fit in her backpack. But Alicia didn't want to argue about what she knew and instead focused on getting ready. This time they had the luxury of being able to plan a bit more, and she would have an actual sleeping bag. *Ohhh, so much better than just sleeping on the ground!*

Let's see, what else, Alicia thought. *Knife, flashlight, jacket, towel, matches.* Oh . . . wait! Alicia suddenly realized that she actually didn't need matches. She could use her magic to create fire. *Amazing!*

She grabbed trail mix and breakfast bars. *I'm sure Dad's bringing them, but it's good to have extra,* she thought. *They don't weigh much, and I've got space.*

"Alright, I'm ready," she declared, looking over to see if her father was as well. He smiled up at her from the lower bunk bed, where he was busy pulling on his hiking shoes.

"I'm ready, too," he said. Alicia watched as her father stood up and performed a small up-and-down bouncing movement, wiggling his toes to make sure his shoes fit comfortably. "Let's load up the car."

They gathered their backpacks and sleeping bags and headed outside. Tawny was still lying in a patch of particularly bright sunlight, her fur becoming dustier than normal from the drying dirt. She raised her head, her eyes tracking the two as they walked to the car.

Alicia opened the back door of the brown sedan and tossed her gear inside. Then looking back at the cougar, she returned and knelt by the cat, stroking her sun-warmed flank, and feeling the dark smooth scars beneath her fingertips.

"You're going to come with us, right?" she asked as Tawny nuzzled her hand. "I don't think you'd enjoy riding in the car," her voice softened, "and I don't think my dad would enjoy you riding in the car either." The cat blinked slowly and looked at the vehicle as if she understood. "But we are going to see Thunderbolt. I'm sure you know the way, right?"

At the mention of her former master's name, Tawny rose to her feet, shaking the dust from her in a cloud that made Alicia cough and back away. The cat stretched both front paws out together, lowering her head to the ground in that way all cats do, repeated the motion with each hind leg individually, then stood there, waiting.

Alicia knelt and gave the cougar's fuzzy ears one last scratch and watched the big cat turn away. Tawny moved off into the woods, heading north toward the tall mountain the Ancient called his home. The low bushes closed gently behind her, leaving no trace of the cat's passing.

Rising, Alicia looked back toward the cabin to see her mom standing on the front porch, hands clasped together anxiously, watching her young daughter play with the wild animal. Alicia knew spending time with Tawny was completely safe, but her mom still had difficulty accepting that. Alicia was feeling too excited for the trip to continue to hold a grudge about her mom's inability to trust her judgment, so she ran up the steps to the porch and threw her arms around her mother.

"I'm going to prove to you and Dad that everything I've told you is true," she promised. "And I'm going to try and fix this mess I've created." Alicia knew delivering on the first thing would be the easy part. She wasn't so sure about the second.

Her father finished getting his gear packed in the car. Slapping

Pancakes, Preparations, & Promises

the car roof, he called out, "Let's go, Lish!"

"Alright," she called back, her voice muffled by her mom's embrace. Alicia gave her mother a final squeeze before turning away. In her haste to get to the car, she practically tripped over her fast-growing feet. Flinging open the passenger door, she jumped into the front seat, buckling herself in tightly.

"We'll be back soon, hon," Richard said to his wife. "And hopefully, have an explanation for all of this."

"I hope so too," Kate said. "I love you both. Please take care and stay safe." Waving to them, a half-smile on her face, she added, "Oh, and Richard?"

"Yes?"

"Try not to let her burn down the forest."

"MO-om," Alicia complained, shouting through the rolled-down passenger window. "I heard that!"

"Just so long as you understood it as well," Kate shot back. "I love you both."

Richard opened his door and climbed into the driver's seat, patting Alicia on the leg as he settled in. "You ready?"

"Yep," she said.

"Then let's get this show on the road." He started the car and put it into gear. As they rolled down the driveway, Alicia turned and looked back at her mom, still standing on the porch and waving. A layer of dust coated the car's rear window, distorting her mom's features and making it difficult for Alicia to recognize her mother.

Alicia quickly waved back, then wiggled herself around, watching the road ahead and preparing for what she falsely expected to be a quick adventure.

 Magic in the Blood

Pancakes, Preparations, & Promises

As the car rolled past the end of the driveway and on, Alicia and her father both failed to notice the mound of roots just off the left side of the road. They probably would not have given it much thought, even if they had seen it. More of a curiosity to think about later. The mound was about the size of a watermelon split lengthwise.

And it had not been there the night before.

3

CHANGES

The drive to Thunderbolt's mountain should have been fairly simple and short. By car, it wasn't really that far from the cabin, not more than thirty minutes or so to reach the trail that led up the mountain. The dirt road was wide and smooth, lined on either side with bushes, wildflowers, skunk cabbage, and thistles. Squirrels would dart out ahead of them, freezing for a moment before scampering across to the other side or changing their minds and returning to where they came from. Occasionally, her father would need to tap the brakes when a particular squirrel decided he was just too confused by the big car coming toward him to move one way or another.

Alicia cranked down her window, allowing the chilled, pine-scented air to roll in and chase away the musty smell of the enclosed car. The breeze caught her hair, lifting and blowing it about her head.

The coming winter had already changed the woods from a uniform green to a mix of Thanksgiving-like colors, shades of orange, yellows, reds, and browns. The tamarack trees had turned a vivid yellow, poking up like giant candlesticks among the dark green lodgepole pines and spruce.

Alicia watched the forest pass by, spotting a deer here or there before they bounded away into the trees to be hidden from view. She kept her eyes peeled for other wildlife, but nothing else was seen. Overall, it should have been a pleasant drive all the way to the point at which the hiking trail began. At least, that's how it was supposed to be.

 Changes

Things had . . . *changed* . . . since the barrier came down. While Alicia had already noticed how the world appeared much more colorful and beautiful, what became clearer to her was that what once were two separate worlds had now combined. Overlapping and merging in unexpected ways. She thought that if she had been able to take two identical pictures from the exact same location, but a hundred years apart, and then print those pictures out on transparent paper and lay them on top of each other, that might represent exactly what she was seeing. The result of this overlap became more and more apparent, fantastical, and disturbingly unreal the farther they drove from the cabin and the closer they got to where the barrier had once been.

Maybe it was the fact that they were driving away from land that was more developed, where people lived and had cabins, deeper into the wilderness. Still, Alicia began to see some very odd visuals. Up ahead, a tree had split in half about ten feet from its base, at which point it became two completely different trees. And it was not simply a tree that had divided into two trunks, a somewhat common sight in the forest. No, what she was seeing was two completely different *species* of trees, one pine, and one aspen!

Alicia glanced over at her father in amazement. He returned the look, and she knew he had also seen it. Staring out her open window, she saw bushes with strange mixes of flowers growing within their branches. It was like looking at a bouquet you might find at a florist with a little plastic "Get Well" or a "Happy Anniversary" sign poking out. There were orange Indian Paintbrush blossoms with white daisies sprouting from the same plant and a yellow Black-eyed Susan thrown in the mix as well. None of it made sense, and she felt an increasing unease at the randomness of it all.

The road they traveled wasn't spared the confusion either. As they drove up the windy mountain road, the surface went from being open and clear to being slowly overtaken by weeds, or having boulders blocking their lane, becoming more like a wide, wild trail than a place for cars. At one point, after coming around a narrow curve, a tree was growing right in the middle of the road, causing her dad to shout out and come to a complete stop before driving slowly forward, maneuvering his way around the obstacle.

Alicia finally saw new wildlife and wished she hadn't. There stood one of the big squirrel-like marmots that roamed the forest in abundance, squat and fuzzy. Except in reality, what she saw was really only half a marmot. The back half. She could see the fat rodent's rear legs and brownish fur leading up to its chest, where it connected with a large stone. There was blood on the stone as if it had suddenly appeared, severing the poor thing in half. Alicia could see that the remains of the animal had begun to decay, with dark flies buzzing, and trails of ants collecting a gory feast to take back to their queen. Alicia looked quickly away. It was one of the most horrible things she had ever seen.

With the changes to the road, her father was forced to drive much more slowly. Every dusty turn, as they twisted their way higher and higher into the hills above the north end of the lake, brought something bizarre to see. And the road itself was no longer smooth or level. Large potholes dotted the ground, and the small hills and valleys her father had to drive around or gently over kept his hands gripping the steering wheel like iron bands. If the road had been paved, the asphalt would have been cracked, crumbled, and destroyed.

What they had expected to be a short drive had suddenly become its own challenge, and it took them over two hours to travel the distance from their cabin to the hiking trail. Her father weaved and dodged the vehicle around things that didn't belong.

Arriving at the trailhead, Alicia could see the wooden sign that marked the trail, but it was only half there. The other half was simply gone, as if it had never existed. "Here . . . the trail . . . Thunder . . ." was written in white block letters on a brown board, with an arrow stamped into the wooden sign below the words, pointing up the hill and to the north.

Alicia's dad pulled the car into a bare patch, free of brush, along the side of what had become a weed-choked path. He practically leaped out of the car, stretching and flinging his arms wildly. The tension he had been under during the last thirty minutes of the drive, never knowing what they might see next, had cramped up his shoulders, the muscles there tight as guitar strings, and he needed to shake it off before continuing.

Alicia scrambled out of the car as well, and paused a moment to look around, seeing the weirdness of the forest reaching extreme levels this far from the cabin. A small sapling was growing straight through a large chunk of granite, its sap slowly leaking away around the base, where organic met mineral, and streaming in thin rivulets over the sides of the rock, like a candle left burning forgotten in its holder. It reminded her of her abandoned pancakes and the syrup dripping from the stack, and she felt her stomach clench in hunger.

Looking down, waiting for the pain to go away, Alicia saw the most beautiful wildflower growing at her feet. It had petals of different shapes and colors, some yellow, others white, and a single orange one that was larger than the rest. She reached down to touch the flower gently, and the orange petal broke loose, falling to the ground and turning to dust as fine as the powder on a butterfly's wings. As if it had never belonged there in the first place.

Her stomach relaxed and Alicia heard the soft, tinkling chimes of a small stream nearby. Going to investigate and hoping to get a quick sip, she found the water flow ran smack into an old stump, splashing randomly in different directions, not yet finding a new course to start forming. The sight made her uncomfortable and she left it alone. Like the orange flower petal that turned to dust, she felt as if she did not belong here.

"What is going on?" her father asked loudly, slowly turning in circles, perplexed at what he saw all around him.

"I don't know," Alicia said, "but I think it might have something to do with the way time moved at different speeds in the two realms. It caused each world to grow and change in its own way, at its own pace." She was trying to make sense of what she was seeing. "When I explored the Wild Side, everything was overgrown and the entire world looked much more primeval than ours does, reclaimed by nature when humans were banished. I think that when the barrier came down, and the two worlds merged, Nature tried her best. This is what we got."

"It's so bizarre. And creepy, too." Alicia watched her father begin to pace back and forth, looking distraught, trying to shake off an unnatural feeling and a growing sense that not everything was as normal as he had believed.

It disturbed Alicia to see her father like this, and she watched him with a small frown on her face. She had always imagined him as strong, able to face anything. She once saw him chase a bear up a tree and thought he was the bravest person that ever lived. In her mind, she would always see him as a kind of Superman, but for the first time, she was also seeing him as Clark Kent. As someone mortal.

"It's ok, Dad," Alicia said, trying to be reassuring. After all, she had seen much worse in her explorations of the Wild Side. He stopped moving and looked at her.

"How can you say that?" He gestured toward one of the many strange two-species trees. "That is not ok! That is not normal!"

Alicia paused, not wanting to argue. "I know it's a lot," she continued. "Between both of my visits, I've had a lot of time to process and accept some of this strangeness. It was all terrifying but wondrous at the same time."

His brow furrowed and mouth clenched, her father continued to look at her, and Alicia saw she had his attention. "On our hikes, you always introduced me to new discoveries that, to you, were commonplace, but for me as a kid, were incredible, strange, and exciting. There are places in these woods that will be magical to me for as long as I live because of that." Gesturing around them, gracefully pointing at flowers, trees, and multicolored rocks. "Now it's my turn to share with you some of the wonders of *this* place."

Her father stared at her for a long moment before looking up and taking it all in as if seeing the forest for the first time. He looked back at her with an expression she didn't quite recognize. Confusion?

"When did you grow up so much?" he asked. "What happened to my little girl?"

"It's this place," she said. "It kinda forces you to grow up and learn to fend for yourself. And . . ." pulling a hand away, she snapped her fingers, lighting a fire in her hand. ". . . it changes you," she finished with a sly smile.

"Put that out," he groaned. Alicia shook her hand, extinguishing the flames, a little embarrassed by her display but continuing to smile inwardly at her ability.

Recovering from the momentary shock of seeing the magic, her father said, "Thank you, Lish. I was losing my head there for a moment" waving his free hand around, echoing his daughter's movement a few minutes ago. "But if your stories are true, and you survived all . . . *this*. Then I suppose together, we can as well."

"Hey, you shouldn't have doubted me," Alicia said with satisfaction. "The stories are true, alright. You'll see."

Together, they gathered their gear from the car. With some help from her dad, Alicia shrugged on her backpack and got the sleeping bag strapped securely on her back. He did the same himself.

Now that they had calmed down a bit, he looked around again. "What's the first thing we need to do?" he asked.

"Find the perfect walking stick!" she exclaimed, knowing this was always the most important step before setting out on any hike.

"Exactly."

And so that's what they did.

4

VOICES ON A MOUNTAIN TRAIL

The trail going up the mountain was well-defined, even with the two worlds merged, so hiking didn't take a lot of effort. Alicia remembered using an established deer trail during her earlier visit. She guessed that in what she was calling the normal world—her world—people had made the hiking trail on top of the existing path that had already been cleared by animals, so when the realms merged, there was little difference between the two.

They walked single file, her father leading the way, sometimes passing between large boulders or around trees, other times through small, open meadows that filled the air with the most amazing scents of late-blooming wildflowers, a multitude of butterflies flitting between blossoms. Alicia would use her walking stick to carefully push aside any of the thorny plants, careful not to disturb the bees she saw zipping around in search of nectar. Together she and her father, like the bees, zigged and zagged a gentle course up the mountainside.

As the morning progressed, the temperature warmed significantly, with a cloudless and beautiful blue sky above. Father and daughter were fortunate to have such nice weather this late in the season. Alicia pushed up her shirt sleeves as a light sweat began to form on her face and neck from the exertion of the hike. The trail wasn't challenging yet; it was just a gradual uphill climb at this point. But she knew from experience it would get much steeper as they got closer to the top.

For now, Alicia and her father settled into a comfortable rhythm of walking for fifteen minutes or so, then taking a break to sip cool water from their canteens and take in their surroundings. They continued to see the oddities produced by the two worlds colliding, blending elements like a collage of photos except in real life. A butterfly with different colored wings. A mashup of organic and in-organic like the tree-stone they saw earlier. And most horrible of all, a large deer, with the legs and tail of a fox dangling from the side of its narrow chest. The deer bounded away, emitting squeals of pain, while the fox bits flopped up and down, leaking something wet. The unnaturalness of it made Alicia ill, so she began to avert her eyes from the strange shapes and angles when she saw them.

How far does this corruption extend into my world, she thought. Beyond the lake, the forest? Maybe there are whole cities with trees growing through buildings. Or rivers emerging from nowhere to smash into the sides of houses, sweeping away cars and people unlucky enough to be in their paths. The sense of responsibility was almost overwhelming for the teen. Alicia did not know if the two worlds could ever find a balance, which filled her with a sense of urgency to find a solution and restore the barrier she had broken. Maybe there was none to be found.

The sun shone down warmly from above Alicia and her father as they hiked, captivated by the colors around them. Most of the pine trees were bold, dark green, but some had shed their summer hue, transitioning from green to a bright yellow, the color of flame, that they carried through winter. So had the thick bushes, laying low to the ground. The fall colors stood out in stark contrast to the typical shades of green. Everything had a freshly washed appearance, like the way the world almost looks plastic when the sun comes out after a heavy rainstorm.

They walked mostly without talking, except for the occasional moment of excitement to point out a hawk circling above or a harmless garter snake crossing the path in front of them, searching for field mice. She decided that from the point of view of the mice, the snake wasn't so harmless. But that was part of nature, and she tried not to dwell on it for too long.

As she walked, Alicia swung her walking stick like a sword severing the long stalks of grass that grew alongside the path. Sometimes she dragged it behind her, letting the tip draw a line in the dirt marking their passage, like crumbs the children had left on the path to the witch's gingerbread house. She didn't really need it much at this point, with the trail still being fairly easy. And the walking stick wasn't like a wand, as she had previously thought. Alicia had learned she did not need a wand to do magic.

During her last visit to the Wild Side, Gran'Tree, the great yellow pine, had suggested magic was contained in her long-lost walking stick, abandoned at the base of the great tree three years prior. But that had not been the truth, not really. Yes, the lost stick brought forth the magic again. But the truth was, it had been within her sleeping the whole time. She just needed that reminder to reawaken it.

Did that make *her* the witch of that classic fairy tale? She had no desire to eat children. *Not yet, anyway, mwaa ha ha*, she thought and giggled quietly.

It was still comforting to carry the walking stick right now, even if she didn't have to rely on it for support quite yet. It was a tradition on hikes. And some traditions were worth keeping.

In the quiet of the journey (at least as "quiet" as a forest can be

with birds calling, squirrels chattering, and other wildlife creeping through the brush, creating a constant variety of sounds), Alicia heard snippets of what sounded like voices. Like hearing a radio playing in another room where the dial wasn't properly tuned to the station, so the words kept fading in and out between the static. The voices, if that was what they really were, were too hushed and muffled to understand clearly. It could have just been her imagination translating the random noises of the forest, or the burbling of a nearby stream, into something that sounded sort of like speaking.

"It is her."

". . . she is . . . back."

". . . the One . . ."

"Dad, do you hear that?" Alicia asked.

Her father stopped walking and listened. Alicia was so distracted and intent on trying to decipher what she was hearing that she bumped right into him.

"Whoa, whoa, hey, I've got you," he said as he caught her from falling over.

"Oww!" she said, rubbing her face in annoyance as if it was his fault she hadn't been paying attention. "Tell me when you're going to stop."

"Well, excuse me, little lady."

"*Little lady?*" Alicia began to fume. He was going to answer for that.

"What do you hear?" he asked before she could say anything.

Alicia decided to get back to that comment later. They both waited and listened for a moment. "It's like voices. But not loud or clear. I can't really understand what they are saying. Just a random word here and there."

They sat still a minute more, straining to hear whatever sounds they could. But all that came back to them was the soft susurration of the wind blowing gently through the treetops. The voices, if they ever existed, were gone.

Alicia had the urge to snap her fingers, calling forth the fire and breaking the silence. It was a habit she had developed since rediscovering her magic, and it oddly gave her comfort. Plus, Alicia knew it would irritate her dad, which would be a bonus right now. But she resisted the temptation.

"I guess it was nothing," she said. "Let's just keep going." Alicia pushed past her father and headed up the trail, increasing her walking speed. She remembered from her previous journey up this mountain that they still had a long way to go before even reaching the canyon crossing, and the day was not slowing in its progression. Their plan was to camp by the canyon for the night, as there was a large, clear patch of ground to build a campfire and lay out their sleeping bags. They didn't want to cross the gap in the dark, especially now, not knowing what changes the merge might have brought.

"Let the great adventure continue!" her father roared loudly behind her. She looked over her shoulder to see him throwing his hands in the air and waving his stick like a Neanderthal with a bone, startling a couple of nearby robins from their ground foraging, causing them to take flight to some low tree branches.

Alicia turned away, rolling her eyes and scoffing in derision. *Such a child*, she thought. While she used to laugh at such antics, as a teenager getting ready to go into high school, she had little tolerance for what she saw as "dad" behavior and now just found it embarrassing. She was thankful none of her friends were around to see it.

Alicia heard her dad's quick steps on the packed dirt as he jogged to catch up with her. She kept her left hand on the walking stick, and her right hand jammed into her pants pocket so she wouldn't be tempted to click her fingers.

5

A GRUESOME DISCOVERY

Shadows from the trees began to lengthen as the sun passed overhead and slowly descended to the west. The air gradually turned cooler as the afternoon turned into early evening. Shirt sleeves came down, moist, with saggy wrists from where they had stretched, collecting sweat while pushed higher on arms throughout the day.

As they continued to hike, Alicia began to notice several strange mounds randomly scattered throughout the forest. The mounds appeared to be small sticks woven together in a tight latticework. They ranged in size from a baseball to larger duffel bag-sized piles. She had never seen anything like them before and thought they might be intricately constructed anthills. The nature lover in her knew ants would make large homes out of pine needles, but from a distance, these appeared to be more advanced than that. Some ground-dwelling bird nests perhaps?

Alicia pointed them out to her dad and asked about them, but he didn't recognize them either. The piles were a little too far off the path to call for further investigation, and she concluded the mounds were just one more result of the mixed-up worlds.

At some point, Alicia caught the movement of something large and golden behind the trees. She saw that Tawny had finally caught up with them to join the journey. Alicia also caught that her father had noticed as well, seeing an extra tightness in his shoulders that wasn't due to carrying a backpack and bag all day. He was still clearly not comfortable with the closeness of the big cat.

A Gruesome Discovery

Tawny kept her distance from the pair but stayed within eyesight. The big cat felt protective of the young girl and wanted to remain near enough to shield her from potential threats. Not that there was anything to be afraid of just now, but night was approaching, and the cat had not forgotten the wolf attack only a few short weeks ago. Alicia hadn't forgotten it either and could still remember vividly the intense pain in her scalp as the wolf had tried to drag her away from camp, her hair clamped firmly in its long teeth. If not for Tawny . . . she did not want to think about that.

The trees were beginning to thin out, growing farther and farther apart, as if the rest of the thick forest had decided to pick up and move, leaving a few stragglers behind. Alicia knew she and her dad were getting close to the clearing where they would set up camp, which was good, considering the slow shadow of night creeping in along the eastern edge of the sky. Even now, if she listened closely, she could hear the faint sound of the river rushing swiftly in the depths of the canyon, sending up a quiet roar like the constant hum of voices in a crowded room, which echoed lightly through the darkening woods.

In no time, they arrived at the site and shrugged off their packs, stretching their arms and legs, working out the stiffness that was beginning to settle there. Alicia reached into her bag and pulled out the trail mix. She had been hungry since starting the hike, her half-eaten breakfast long digested by now, but disoriented and ill at the same time from the sights they had seen. Now her hunger was back with a vengeance.

Alicia dug into the bag with gusto, grabbing one handful after another, and shoveling the collection of nuts, raisins, and chocolate chips into her mouth. Stuffing the plastic baggie back into her pack, she pulled out her canteen, taking several big swigs before dropping everything to the ground. She began her search of the clearing, scanning for stones large enough to create a fire pit but not so large she couldn't lift them.

Alicia noticed her father observing her and was proud to be able to prove her efficiency. *They thought I needed a chaperone, ha!* There was no monkey business. She went straight to work on the task at hand, suspecting that he probably thought she'd laze about and let him do all the work. Instead, Alicia took to the job swiftly using the practiced skills she had employed these past several weeks.

"Dad, I could use some help," Alicia said, lifting another heavy rock, carrying it back, and adding it to the other stones she had already hauled and placed, beginning to form a ring for the campfire.

"Oh yeah, sorry. I was just lost in thought." Her dad began searching for more stones, finding a few bigger ones. The two of them closed the circle quickly with just enough light left to gather dead branches and other kindling for the fire.

Expanding her search to a wider area, looking for sticks and dead tree limbs to burn, Alicia almost tripped over one of the strange mounds she had noticed earlier. Kneeling down, she peered more closely at the pile, this one about the size of a basketball. She used one of the sticks she was carrying to tap the mound a couple of times on top, *tap tap*, to see if ants would come scurrying out to defend their hill from the intruder. Nothing happened.

Tawny had been wandering close by and now approached the girl, curious about what she had found. Alicia felt the weight of the cat settling in beside her, pressing against her leg. Tawny leaned

A Gruesome Discovery

forward and sniffed the mound, immediately pulling her head back. The fur on her neck bristled, and a low, deep growl rumbled from her throat. Alicia thought it almost sounded like a purr but knew anyone hearing that kind of purr was probably moments away from something extremely painful happening to them, likely involving a lot of blood being spilled.

"What's wrong, girl?" Alicia asked. "It's only a pile of sticks."

The growl continued, and the golden cat slowly took a step back, looking from Alicia to the pile and back, her great yellow eyes showing concern. Clearly, she was warning, *step away, step away*, but Alicia couldn't see what the problem was. Maybe there was a snake under the pile, which could make sense. Alicia knew there were not any venomous snakes in the forest, but perhaps the great cat just didn't like serpents.

Alicia tapped the mound again with her stick, harder this time, *TAP*, hoping that if there *was* a snake there, she would chase it away, but still, nothing happened. "I don't think there's anything to worry about," she told the cat. "And this could make great firewood."

Setting her collected sticks down, Alicia reached out and placed her hands on the mound. Tawny lowered herself, preparing to pounce should anything bad happen.

Alicia felt something odd beneath her fingertips. A kind of vibration of sorts, as if the mound were some type of machine and what she felt was the gears moving within. The mound's surface was cold and rough, yet she got the sense that it was alive somehow, or at least had been very recently.

Alicia grabbed tightly, her slender fingers finding purchase between the numerous sticks that made up the mound, and she tugged. It wiggled the tiniest bit but stuck to the ground, like a bush, its roots maintaining a hold on the earth beneath it. Alicia pulled harder and still could not free it from the soil. She stood up, bumping Tawny, who continued to growl softly beside her. Reaching down, she pulled as hard as she could but still did not have the strength to lift the mound of sticks free.

Now she was determined. Alicia was not going to let this pile of sticks get the best of her. Admittedly, curiosity was also getting to her. She had to know what this thing was, and it seemed the only way to find out was to somehow pull it loose.

Looking around, she found a good-sized stone and a thick branch, long and sturdy. She jammed the end of the branch under the pile of sticks and, using both hands, lifted the stone and hammered at the end she was holding, forcing the branch deeper under the mound. Then she wedged the stone under the branch about halfway between where it was buried beneath the mound and the other end, now pointing up at an angle.

With her quickly devised fulcrum in place, she went to the high end of the branch sticking up into the air and pulled down with all her might, feeling the rough bark dig into the soft flesh of her fingers. The dead branch was thick and strong, and Alicia felt the smallest bit of movement coming from the buried end. Changing positions, she forced the branch down, pushing now instead of pulling, practically climbing on it with all her weight.

With a steady tearing sound, like two pieces of Velcro being pulled slowly apart, the mound gradually came free from the earth. Alicia reduced her force, and suddenly the bundle of sticks flipped over onto its domed top like a turtle upended.

A Gruesome Discovery

Alicia dropped the branch and moving closer, saw what appeared to be milky white worms, or vines, in the dirt where the mound originally rested. In the fading light, the soil appeared reddish in color. The worms thrashed back and forth as if searching for something and then withdrew, disappearing quickly into the ground.

Without warning, Alicia's nostrils were ravaged by the smell! Such a stench of death and decay, sweetly sour and heavy, rose from the pile of sticks in a cloud that assaulted her senses, causing her eyes to water.

"UGH!" she huffed, quickly pulling the sweaty collar of her shirt up to cover her mouth and nose, holding it tightly in place with her left hand. Tawny backed away, swiping at her own nose with her paw, trying to get rid of the offending smell that filled the air.

Curiosity winning out, Alicia breathed through her mouth to try and reduce the terrible stink and moved slowly forward to peer into the mess of sticks. She didn't know what she was looking at, at first. A wooden shell filled with fur, skin, blood, and bones in a shriveled mess. Then horror overtook her as she saw the long gray ear of a jackrabbit curled around the inner edge.

The poor creature had been trapped inside this pile of sticks, and the . . . what . . . worms? . . . had been feeding on it like maggots. Drinking its insides, or so it appeared, as only the shell of the animal remained, collapsed and empty, like the husk of an insect after a spider has fed. Alicia had a vision of one of the juice boxes that she used to love so much. When it was empty, she'd continue sucking on the straw, trying to get every last bit out while the sides of the cardboard container collapsed. That is what this reminded her of. The thought filled her with disgust. She did not think she would ever be able to look at another one of those juice boxes again.

Her father heard Alicia's exclamation and approached, questioning and making a horrid face. "Oh wow," he said, waving his hand in front of his nose. "Did you find something dead?"

"Yeah, you could say that," she answered, her voice muffled through her shirt and hand. Pointing with her free hand, she said, "Remember all those mounds of sticks we saw? Well, that's one of them, but I don't understand it."

Her dad quickly looked at the mess in front of her, saw the contents of the shell of sticks, and stepped back. Tawny was also standing close by, but it didn't seem to matter as much to Richard, with this new, disgusting thing grabbing his attention.

"Is that a rabbit in there?" he asked.

"Yeah, I think so."

He took another step away. "Come on, Lish. Leave it," he said softly, a wary note of caution in his voice. "Let's get back to camp and get that fire going before it gets much colder."

Alicia felt a chill in her arms, too, though she wasn't sure if it was from the night coming on or the thing on the ground in front of them and the thought of disgusting, pale, blood-sucking worms.

The trio backed away, feeling uneasy, leaving the pile of sticks and its gruesome treasure to the flies that were now beginning to gather. There was no way Alicia was using *that* for firewood. What came from Mother Nature, let it be reclaimed by her.

The cycle of life goes on.

6

THE BURNING GIRL

Alicia and her father sat on opposite sides of the campfire ring, staring into the small blaze in front of them. Orange embers floated up into the air, glowing for a moment before winking out of existence. They reminded Alicia of Vulcan's army of sprites, the Ancient's eyes and ears throughout the woods. Alicia had seen the dots of color drifting between the trees as she and her father had gotten the campfire burning. She glanced away from the fire now, looking for them but seeing no sign of the small beings. Alicia looked back to the fire and wondered if the Ancient was still watching her. And if so, why?

The dinner with her father had consisted of more trail mix and berries they had foraged along the path. "We're basically bears," Alicia said as she shoveled another handful of berries into her mouth, grinning. During their hike, they had gathered a couple of plastic baggies full, which they had brought along just for that purpose. The two now sat hypnotized by the flickering flames, resting on their unrolled sleeping bags, their tongues dyed purple from their juicy meal.

"What do you think that was?" she asked her father, breaking the silence that had settled over them after dinner.

Alicia watched his face lit by the yellow flames reflecting in his brown eyes. He appeared lost in thought, and she was not sure if he had heard her question.

Her father had, and knew what she was asking about. But he didn't have an immediate answer. He was still wondering the same thing.

"Do you think it has something to do with the other world merging with ours?" she asked, a bit louder this time, attempting to grab his attention.

"I don't know," he finally responded. "You've been to this . . . what did you call it . . . *Wild Side*. Have you ever seen anything like that?"

"Never," she replied. "And I definitely saw some weird things. But that seemed to me almost—I don't know—evil. I mean, was that rabbit put in that trap on purpose? So cruel!" Alicia shook her head. "And who would have done that? And what else has been trapped? We saw a ton of those mound things today, some of them a lot bigger too. Bigger than rabbit-sized . . ."

The questions poured from her, and she shivered with the thought of somebody capturing animals and feeding them to the worms. *What would be the point?*

"It seriously gives me the creeps." Her voice trailed off as she reached out to put a hand on Tawny, stroking the coarse fur and taking comfort from the cat. The cougar had come closer to be near the fire and the girl. The cat, too, had been disturbed by the unknown thing. Her father, who had been sitting close, scowled and scooted away to where he now sat. But Alicia didn't care. She loved the beast, and her father would just have to learn to deal with it.

"Truth be told, it kind of gives me the creeps, too," he said. "And you're right, there *were* bigger mounds. That thought makes me *very* uncomfortable." He took off his shoes, setting them nearby, unzipped his sleeping bag, and scooched down inside. "I think I'll have a hard time falling asleep with that image in my head."

Alicia glanced over at her dad, his eyes open and staring blankly into the night sky. She looked back to the fire, watching yellow turn to orange turn to red. Her mind was spinning with thoughts of what she had seen today. All of the strangeness. And thoughts of her own magic, which was kind of cool, but also seemed to come with its own responsibilities. She had attempted to start the campfire by snapping her fingers, but her father would have none of that. Her gaze slid back to her father. *He'd* brought matches and was going to use those matches like a normal person.

Normal? Alicia thought, her brow furrowing. *Am I no longer normal because I have magic? Have I ever been normal? And now, do I need to hide my magic from the world?* She almost wanted things to go back to how they were, when she didn't know about the Wild Side. Mostly, anyway. *I'd like to keep the magic for a little while.*

Heavy thoughts for a girl not even in high school yet, but these are what weighed her down and crawled into the sleeping bag with her, along with the chilly night air. She lay on her side and stared into the dying embers. After a moment, she felt the warm press of Tawny against her back as the cat protectively curled up close to her.

Tomorrow, she would meet Thunderbolt for the second time. And this time, she wouldn't let him lock himself away without giving her the answers she deserved.

A sharp snarl dragged Alicia up from the depths of sleep she did not think she would be able to achieve. The clearing was dark, but a soft glow was still coming from the campfire embers, and it took a moment for her eyes to adjust to the dim light. Fighting against the grogginess, she blinked eyelids that felt three times heavier than they should, pulled back the edge of her sleeping bag, and pushed herself up on one elbow to search for the source of the continuing growl. It was coming from Tawny, who was standing close by and appeared to be snapping at one of her large front paws.

"What's happening?" She heard her father grumble and looked to see him faintly in the dark on the other side of the coals, sitting up and eyeing the cat.

"I don't know," Alicia replied sleepily, looking back at the cougar. "Tawny's got something on her paw that's bothering her."

Alicia watched as the great cat alternated between snapping at her paw and tugging it. It seemed stuck to the ground, but she couldn't be sure in the darkness.

Looking about, her brain still foggy from sleep, Alicia searched for a way to help but realized that since she didn't know what was wrong, she had no idea what could be done. And from the sounds she was making, Tawny may be injured. Alicia was always taught never to bother a hurt animal and to get help. Even a pet could lash out or bite when in pain.

As her eyes continued to adjust to the dark, Alicia saw a stick poking up through the outside edge of her sleeping bag down by her leg and thought, *that's strange*. She must have unrolled her bag right on top of it in the fading light of the previous evening without even noticing. She did not remember seeing it and certainly hadn't felt it with her feet.

Studying the area, she suddenly realized the stick was moving on its own, as if alive. It lengthened and then bent, the tip leaning toward the side and beginning to curl down. Alicia felt so confused. *What magic is this?*

The stick (she clearly saw, even in the moonlit darkness, that it was wooden and not a worm or snake or something) continued to bend down. Alicia stared, fascinated by the movement, half convinced she was dreaming. Her eyes tracked the tip like a cobra watching a snake charmer play his flute. Suddenly, and with an unexpected burst of speed, the end of the stick drove down through the middle of her sleeping bag, scraping along the inside of her ankle and plunging into the earth, trapping her leg tightly against the ground! Seconds later, she felt a stab of pain underneath her leg, as if a giant thorn had pricked her calf.

"OUCH!" she screamed and tugged her leg, but it held fast inside her sleeping bag. Another stick ripped through the top of the sleeping bag, curving over and plunging down, creating a second binding around the same leg.

Seeing Alicia struggling but not understanding, her dad climbed out of his bag and moved quickly to her side. "Dad, help!" Alicia yelled. "I'm stuck!" He reached down, grabbed her by the armpits, and pulled, adding his strength to hers, yanking her halfway out of the sleeping bag and dragging both backwards, breaking free of the sticks.

Alicia quickly kicked off the sleeping bag from where it remained tangled around her feet as her dad helped her to stand. Snapping her fingers, she summoned flames that lit the area around her with an orange glow. Her father took a quick step away.

She tugged her pant leg with her free hand and craned her neck to look behind her. Alicia could see a small hole in the back of her leg oozing a slow trickle of blood. Feeling the sting, she sucked air sharply through her teeth as she dropped her pant leg back down.

Tawny was still struggling, snarling at her paw as she fought

to free herself. With the light of the fire in her hand, Alicia could see several of the sticks encasing the cat's paw like a wooden glove. More began climbing up Tawny's leg like ivy spiraling up a tree.

Before Alicia could react, three vine-like sticks aggressively burst from the ground below her. No longer slow and stealthy, these bent and quickly wrapped tightly around her sock-covered feet. At the same time, dozens more of the strange sticks rose under her father's feet, like the tentacles of some underground squid, locking him in place as well.

"What's going on?" he shouted, confused. Alicia watched him reaching down and trying to break the sticks free, but for every one he grabbed, two more appeared, circling his feet and slithering up his legs. He shrieked out in pain and lost his balance, tipping forward and catching himself with his hands. Two more sticks immediately broke free from the dirt in puffs of dust and pine needles, binding his hands to the ground.

Weaving themselves tightly together, Alicia thought as a terrifying recognition dawned on her.

As she stood there in shock, the same thing was happening to her. Alicia felt the stick vines climbing her legs. Another thorn pierced the side of her left heel, causing her to let out a scream, bringing her back to the moment.

Alicia looked down at her body and watched the stick vines reach higher. Shifting her gaze, she watched her father struggling as the stick vines made their way across his back, his face pained while his body arched awkwardly, hands and feet bound to the earth. She turned and watched Tawny do the same, three paws trapped now and one stick vine slowly climbing her flank to slide between her ears and around her head.

She thought about what she had discovered the previous evening. The shell of sticks, the dead rabbit inside, collapsed in on itself, drained of blood, food for the white worms.

"No, no, no, no, no," she started repeating in denial of the situation. Alicia felt intense fear and confusion growing, expanding in her, taking over her thoughts along with the sting of multiple thorns. She didn't understand what this was, how it could be happening, and she felt terrified and helpless. "No, no, no, no!"

Tears of pain and frustration began to stream down her cheeks. They were all going to die! Their bodies hollowed out, consumed by this unknown danger.

"No! No! No! NO! NO!"

"NOOO!"

Alicia wailed into the night, fear taking control, her voice ringing loudly throughout the clearing.

Suddenly, the flames still dancing in her hand flared up, glowing more brightly than ever as if finding a fresh source of fuel. They rushed up her arm, flowing across her chest in a wave, and engulfing her entirely. Alicia's flaming body lit up the clearing and the trees beyond with blazing yellow and orange flames flickering in the night. As she heard a loud crackling sound, the sticks on her legs instantly burned to a crisp, falling away into dark smoke and blackened ash.

Alicia stood freed from the trap, a bright, searing torch chasing the dark. She was an awesome sight to behold.

Without thought, she reached for and grabbed her father's shoulder, pushing and sending her magic his way. The flames raced across his back, over his body, and down his arms and legs, burning away the stick vines.

Richard collapsed to the ground, then rolled away and continued rolling, batting at his clothes with his hands, instinctually working to put out the fire. But as soon as he broke contact with Alicia, the flames covering him were extinguished as if they had never existed, and he felt no pain.

She turned quickly to Tawny, who was held firmly in place, the massive cat's golden eyes wide behind the layer of wood that was forming there. Laying her hands on the cat, Alicia allowed the flames to swath the beast. The armor of sticks quickly charred and burned.

Tawny twisted violently and was free. Instantly, the cougar fled from the girl and fire. The flames disappeared as soon as they were separated, but with ears tucked close, the cat ran fast at a low crouch, putting distance between herself and Alicia, as if still trying to avoid the blaze. Tawny came to a halt at the edge of the clearing, cowering, watching the burning girl intently, frightened by this thing she had become. After a moment, the cougar turned and disappeared into the dark woods.

Alicia looked at her father, on his knees several feet away, and found that he, too, was staring at her, wide-eyed, his mouth hanging open.

Slowly, Alicia raised an arm up in front of her, marveling at the flames that licked and flowed on her skin like water. She let her eyes travel down the length of her body, feeling a smile tug at the corner of her mouth. There was no burning, no pain. She could feel only a gentle, all-encompassing warmth down to her bones, chasing away the cold of the night.

This is new, she thought. *This is power!* She liked it.

Her hand still raised, Alicia looked back first to her dad and then to where the cat had disappeared, both seemingly unnerved by her. This power felt good, natural. It was hers and she wanted it to continue. But the fear she saw in her family, fear of her, felt horrible. Alicia waited a moment longer, relishing the magical feeling. Then concentrating, she pictured the magic collapsing, like turning off a mental faucet, slowly forcing the fire to withdraw.

The flames pulled back from her head. They rolled up her legs from her feet, like an ocean's tide moving in reverse, diminishing and returning until, after a few moments, only her upraised hand was still on fire. The last remaining flames blew away with a final shake of her fingers.

Beneath her, the ground was charred and smoldering. Alicia quickly stamped her feet, smothering any burning spots that remained, returning the clearing to darkness with only the moon and stars shining their light above the final glow from the campfire's last coals.

The attack was over. Whatever just happened, and Alicia had the hint of an idea that she had not quite settled on forming in her head about what it was, thankfully, it was over. Evidently, her show of strength was enough to drive the attack back, for now at least.

Her dad hadn't moved and was still staring up at her.

"Dad. Dad, it's ok. It's me. I'm ok. Are you?" she said.

He looked doubtful but finally closed his mouth. "I, I . . . uh . . . yeah," her dad stuttered softly, confused, at a complete loss for what to say. "I know, yeah, I know. I mean, I guess I know." It sounded like he was trying to convince himself and failing. "I just . . . it's . . .

that was . . ." He stared at the ground and fell silent.

"Yeah, Dad, I know," Alicia replied quietly. "That was new for me as well."

Their eyes, night blind after the brightness of her flames, slowly adjusted to the darkness. They looked around, trying to take in and understand what had just happened.

"Are you ok?" he finally asked, eyes rising to see her again. "Are you hurt or burned?"

"No, I'm not burned," Alicia replied, examining herself or what she could see of herself anyway. "I have some bloody spots on my legs, but nothing serious, I don't think."

"We'll take a look in the morning when it's light," he said, giving Alicia the feeling that, right now, he was scared to approach her. A great sadness filled her at that thought, the idea that her dad might fear her.

"Ok," Alicia said, holding back tears threatening to form.

"What in the world was that?" her father asked. "This is all so new and strange. I mean, has that ever happened? In the Wild Side, I mean."

"No, it hasn't," she said. "Living sticks coming out of the dirt? No, but it looks like we have an answer for what those mounds are. Part of an answer anyway."

And maybe more, she thought but kept that to herself for now.

"There's a large, flat patch of stone over there, nearer to the canyon edge," her dad said, finally standing and pointing. "We should uh . . . probably move our sleeping bags over there. It won't be as soft as the dirt, but possibly . . . I don't know . . . safer, maybe?"

"Yeah, that's a good idea," she said, "Though I don't know if

I'll be sleeping anymore tonight." The unexpected flare-up of the magic in a way she had never experienced before had given her a surge of adrenaline, and now she was wide awake.

Alicia gathered up her torn sleeping bag and followed her father, who was already moving to the hard, flat rock. She spread her bag on the ground and down, feeling the hard stone beneath it but not caring.

Alicia stared up into the sky, watching the billions of stars, remembering the warm magic tingling across her arms. The way it felt. The sense of power it gave her. She had always felt tiny, looking into the vastness of space. Just a pinprick of a person on a pinprick of a planet in an endless universe. But now, in some unidentifiable way, she felt just a little bit bigger.

Alicia closed her eyes. So many thoughts were going through her head now, but one kept coming back over and over again. And the more her mind went there, the more convinced she became.

Gran'Tree.

7
ARGUMENTS & UNDERSTANDINGS

As expected, Alicia and her father had difficulty finding sleep the rest of the night. But they stayed quiet; the two lost in their own thoughts. Alicia couldn't help but wonder what her dad must think of her now, of that explosive show of power. Did he still consider her his daughter, or had she become something else in his mind? A creature changed like this land had changed, not entirely human. Even though she liked the power, maybe even loved it, she felt a little bit like a freak and was afraid to even mention it to her father. Eventually, the adrenaline wore off, and in the crash that followed, Alicia closed her eyes and slept fitfully until morning.

The sky was misty when she woke, water vapor rising from the nearby canyon was clinging to her face and hair. Alicia saw that her dad already had his shoes on and was getting his stuff packed. She looked around, but Tawny was still nowhere to be seen.

"Morning," she said, rubbing her eyes and trying to get her brain working properly. Alicia felt completely wiped out. "Have you seen Tawny?"

"Morning, Lish. Not since last night. She wasn't around when I woke up. Were you able to get any more sleep?"

"A bit," she replied, scanning the clearing for the cat before giving up and rising to her feet. "How about you?"

"Not really. I'm ready to be done with this and get home. I'm starting to worry a bit about your mother. I don't know how far any of this extends."

Arguments & Understandings

Her father sounded tired and scared. Alicia remembered having that same feeling several times during her previous adventures here. "I'm worried too, but we're close now. I have a good feeling we're going to solve this.

"Based on what exactly, Alicia?" He looked at her with eyebrows raised. "Because after last night. After that attack and your . . . whatever it was, it's hard for me to have good feelings about *any* of this!"

"Come on, it's ok," she said, trying to assure him, starting to worry that he would call off the whole trip right then and there. "We'll be back home before nightfall."

Her dad continued looking forlorn as he gathered his gear. *It's ok*, she thought but recognized it was pointless to say anything. *I'll be able to protect us. He'll see.*

Alicia also hoped he wasn't scared of her, but from his comments and the way he looked at her, she was not sure anymore, and that hurt. She assumed—hoped—he just needed time to adapt to this new reality, as did she. Clearly, it had been too much for Tawny, and with all her heart, Alicia prayed the cat wasn't gone for good.

Rolling up her sleeping bag super tight, she walked back over to where she had left her hiking boots the night before. Plopping down, she brushed the dirt and pine needles from her socks the best she could before pulling the worn boots back on. Tugging her pant leg up, she examined the spots where she'd gotten stabbed, but the holes had scabbed over, and the blood had become dry, crusty brown trails down her leg to her sock. She dropped her pant leg, telling herself she would clean it up at the next small stream they found.

Looking up, she saw her dad inspecting his own hands. She could see the small, dried trickles of blood there. He glanced her way, noticed her watching, and nodded to her. She returned the nod as if to say, "Yes, that was bad!"

They dug into their bags and pulled out breakfast bars, two each. Starving, Alicia sank her teeth into the chocolate-encrusted bar. She felt famished and guessed the events of the night had taken their toll on her energy levels. Her dad followed suit, and for a moment, they stopped thinking about all the terrible things that happened yesterday and smiled at each other, enjoying their simple breakfast together.

After finishing their granola bars, they strapped on their gear, double- and triple-checked the campfire to ensure all remaining coals were out and looked at the trail leading to the deep crevasse.

Tawny still hadn't made an appearance. Alicia was not completely surprised, given that, for a moment, she had become a living fireball. Tawny couldn't understand and between that and the attack, of course she was naturally frightened. Alicia's biggest fear was that her unexpectedly powerful use of the magic had scared the cougar off forever. She knew firsthand how shocking it was to see yourself engulfed in flames, even if they didn't burn your skin.

Hoping for the best, Alicia set out on the trail, her father following along. The two of them only had to walk fifty feet or so through the morning mist to the edge of the canyon before she saw that the man-made rope bridge from her world was not there. The Wild Side had completely taken over this space, and only the fallen tree from her last crossing remained.

"We need to cross *that?*" her father asked, looking at the large fallen tree that bridged the narrow canyon before them, its broken base resting on their side while the crown of dead branches lay on

Arguments & Understandings

the opposite side. The sound of the river far below roared up at them. The river that carved its path through this canyon centuries ago was hidden from view by the tops of trees poking up from the mist that clung to them. "I don't think so. We're going to find another way around."

"Dad, I've done it before. Twice! It's not so hard. You just need to be cautious and don't rush."

"Nope, not happening, kiddo. Can you hear that river down there? I don't know how long the fall is, but surviving that is not something I want to test out anytime soon. We'll find another path."

"Come on, Dad, trust me. You were the one who said you were worried about Mom. I am too. If we try to search for another way or need to climb down and back up the other side, we could lose a full day at least! Just watch."

"Alicia, no. Now wait. Wait. Wait!!"

It was too late. Alicia slid down the small drop to the ledge where the close end of the fallen tree rested and was starting to make her way out onto the dew-slicked trunk that crossed the canyon.

She heard her father shout, then mutter something under his breath, probably a bad word, but she didn't care. She would show him it was safe. *As long as you don't look down!*

She heard a tumble of stones behind her and imagined that her dad must have dropped down to the ledge as well, but did not want to look back for fear of losing her balance. The backpack and sleeping bag already set her a little off kilter, so at about the halfway mark, as the trunk began to narrow, she slowly lowered to her hands and knees and crawled the rest of the way across.

Alicia reached the other side uneventfully and maneuvered

through the crown of dead branches like it was some schoolyard jungle gym, carefully avoiding snagging her backpack, to reach the safety of solid ground. She turned to watch her dad, still standing on the other ledge, just glowering at her, one hand on his hip, the other over his chest, feeling his heart race, she imagined.

"Come on, Dad," she called across, raising her voice to be heard over the roar of the river. "You saw me do it. It's safe! Just be careful and crawl like I did if it makes you feel better."

"It doesn't!" he shouted back.

She watched him stand there, lingering, before stepping gingerly out onto the tree, barely lifting his feet with each step, as if he thought his shoes would keep him magnetically attached to the tree.

"That's good, that's good," she called. "Go slow, it can be slippery. And watch out for the broken branch stumps."

He didn't get far, not even five feet, before he dropped to all fours, the motion dragging an audible gasp from Alicia.

"Are you good? You ok?" He didn't respond and her breath quickened, fearing that he would not be able to make it across the gap. "Dad?"

"Alicia, shush!" Her dad sat motionless for a moment, staring at the log below him, licking his lips before beginning to inch forward, sliding his hands across the wet, rough bark.

"That's it, you can do it." Alicia felt like a coach and given her previous experience with the bridge, it wasn't far from the truth. "Just focus on the tree."

Her father followed the advice, watching the tree trunk inch by inch, and trying not to think about what lay out of sight below the tree and the mist rising from the river.

Arguments & Understandings

Alicia watched with hands clenched for several long minutes, finally giving a small squeal as her dad finished the crossing and clambered off, not nearly as graceful as his daughter had. He bent, putting his palms on his knees for a moment.

"You *need* to listen to me, Lish!" he said angrily when he could speak again. "That was dangerous and stupid!"

"It wasn't stupid," she argued back, feeling resentful after she had just helped him cross. She didn't like being called stupid. It wasn't fair. "I told you I did it before. Why can't you just trust me?!" Alicia did not tell him that she had almost fallen before. That would only have complicated her argument. Besides, she had known what to expect and had been more cautious this time.

"Well, it was still dangerous," he shot back, hands on hips, eyeing the tree they had just crossed. "I mean, who knows how long that thing has been there? It could have slipped off the cliff or snapped in two with you out there in the middle!"

"Well, it didn't, did it," she said, defiant. "And now we're on the other side without wasting a whole day!"

Her dad glared at her, then slowly shook his head.

"Fine, I don't want to argue about it. Gimme a second, and we'll keep going."

"Fine." Alicia turned away, feeling unappreciated, looked for her walking stick, and realized she had left it at the campsite. *Well, I didn't want it anyway,* she thought, irritated at her dad. *I should have just come by myself.* What she believed could be a fun trip had turned very sour.

Alicia walked a few steps away, looking up at the last bit of trail they needed to hike. It was steep going from here, and she would actually have preferred to have her walking stick with her now that she thought about it. But she wasn't at all in the mood to go through the tradition of looking for one with her dad, so she stubbornly let the thought go. The faster they got this done, the better.

Richard stepped forward, taking the lead without saying a word, and together they set out on the last stretch to the peak of Thunderbolt, and the Ancient whom the mountain was named for, waiting there.

The final part of the hike was short, maybe a quarter of a mile or less, but it was all uphill. It did not take long to rise above the level of the mist, and the sun was already warming them. Every step of this section was exhausting, as if they were climbing the longest flight of stairs ever.

The pair found a small stream on this side of the canyon, one she was sure eventually followed a path all the way down the mountain to join the river below. They had refilled their canteens and cleaned their wounds. But after all they had been through, they were stopping frequently to rest their aching legs and take small sips of water. Alicia shook her canteen, heard the remaining water slosh inside, and hoped it would last at least until the summit. Thunderbolt must have something to drink, and afterward, coming back down would be less tiring and they could get back to the stream faster to refill.

Alicia continued to see small mounds formed from the stick-vines that had almost trapped them, but there were fewer of them the closer they got to the summit. She had a suspicion of where they

Arguments & Understandings

came from. Alicia had not spoken to her father since leaving the canyon, but this thought was bothering her, and she wanted to talk about it. So, she broke the frustrated silence between them.

"Dad?"

"M'hmm."

"You know those mounds of sticks, and that attack last night?"

"Yeah," he said, showing slightly more interest.

"I think I know what they are. Where they're coming from, I mean." Alicia spoke in short bursts between breaths. Her lungs burned from the exertion of the climb, but she went on, walking with her head down, watching her steps.

"You remember I told you about the big tree."

"Yellow Tree, right?"

"No, Gran'Tree. He was . . . *is* a giant yellow pine."

"That's right," he said, remembering.

"Well, when I went to see him a few weeks ago to find my magic again," she said, "I told him about everything that had happened to me." The sentence came out between breaths "I told him . . . about everything . . . that had . . . happened . . . to me." She paused, taking a drink of water.

"Uh huh?"

"Part of what I told him," she continued, breathing heavily, "was about the attack from The Silver King's pet leeches." Alicia shivered at the thought, despite the heat. "He was the worst of the Ancients. He could somehow absorb my blood through the leeches and wanted it for himself. He wanted to regain his magic by stealing *my* blood."

"Ok. So, you think The Silver King's still after you?" her father asked.

"The thought occurred to me, but no, not anymore. I remembered back to three years ago when I first crossed over. The realm had been afflicted by The Drying. It was Gran'Tree, absorbing all the water supply. He had extended his great roots everywhere throughout the land, not caring for anything but himself and sucking up every bit of moisture he could in the process." She paused, thinking it through, and her father waited for her to continue.

"It's those stick vines that got me thinking. The way they burst from the ground. And when I tore that mound from the dirt, there were all these white things wriggling underneath. I thought they were worms, but they all pulled back into the earth before I got a good look. And the way they burned and turned to ash when touched by my magic. Now, I think they were *roots!* Wooden roots. I think they were Gran'Tree's roots. I think he got the idea from me, and I think that this time, instead of water, he's drinking the blood of animals to grow strong again."

"That's pretty gross," her father said.

"I know, but you should have seen him!" Alicia said. "He was so withered and broken when I last saw him. I almost felt sorry for him. Because of the difference in the flow of time, it had been four thousand years since he had last seen me, and I think that during that time, he grew angry. Terribly angry. I think he longed for the strength he once had. And I think I told him how he could get it."

Richard stopped climbing and turned back to face his daughter. "Alicia, I'm sorry. I admit I was scared earlier, and I got mad." His features softened as he looked at her. "It *was* dangerous crossing that log, but I appreciate your help."

And then he said something Alicia never thought she would hear.

Arguments & Understandings

"I believe you."

He paused to take a drink from the bottle. "You're observant and you've got a good head on your shoulders. I don't know what those things might have been, but you've seen things here that I can't imagine. And look at you, you're a . . . freaking . . . wizard or something."

"A witch!" she said enthusiastically.

"Sure, a witch. Whatever it is, it is beyond my understanding. So, if you think this has something to do with that tree, well, you're the expert here. So, I believe you."

"Thanks, Dad." She stepped forward and gave him a quick hug.

"But we'll have to pick up this conversation later, Lish," he said, stepping back.

"Why?"

"Because we're at the summit."

Alicia looked past her father and saw the crest of the hill beyond. Together they hiked the last few feet and stepped out onto the wide mesa ahead. At the far end sat the wooden shack the Ancient called home.

They had reached Thunderbolt.

And Alicia's world was about to come crashing down.

8

A MEETING WITH DESTINY

Alicia sagged against her father as they stood side-by-side on the summit catching their breath. Her legs were sore and shaky from the hike, and she could feel her shirt sticking to her back beneath the pack. Beads of sweat tickled as they rolled down her neck, like insects crawling across her skin, and she wiped them away.

Alicia was the first to step forward into the clearing, looking around taking in the familiar landscape. She slid her gear off and dumped it on the ground, grabbed the front of her shirt, and flapped it back and forth in the still air, trying to cool down. Alicia had been here only a few weeks ago, but so much had happened since then, it seemed like forever. She did not get the answers she sought then but was determined to get them now.

Before Alicia could call out to Thunderbolt, the door to the little cabin opened wide, and out strolled the Ancient, just as she remembered him. Tall, freakishly so, with long hair and a thick mustache. He looked like he could have stepped directly out of a saloon in the old West. Well, except for the bedclothes that clung to his thin frame. The exact same bedclothes he was wearing the last time she saw him. *Ugh, did he ever wash those things?*

"Alicia. Alicia, my child. You are back," he exclaimed as he hustled across the clearing, smiling. The stink drifting from his clothes was practically visible in the still air. "Oh, I just knew you would return. I just knew it!"

Alicia's father had come up beside her, and leaned forward

extending his hand, looking up at the tall man's face. "Hi, I'm, uh, Richard. Alicia's father. And who are you, exactly?" he asked, though he was fairly sure he already knew the answer to that question.

"Yes, yes. I know who you are," the Ancient replied, ignoring both the extended hand and the question asked by the man attached to that hand. Instead, he placed his own rather large hands on Alicia's thin shoulders. She had to force herself not to grimace from the unwashed smell oozing from Thunderbolt.

"I am so happy to see you. You have done big things! Yes, *very* big things!" He beamed at her with a big horsey, yellowish grin. "You have brought the worlds back together. Is that a good thing? I do not know. After all this time, I do not know."

Thunderbolt seemed almost manic, excited and talkative. Alicia stood immobile, shocked by the behavior of this person, so unlike his previous calm, bored demeanor. This time, he was lively and full of energy. She watched her father let his arm drop when no handshake was offered, and take a step back trying to stretch himself a little taller.

"You've been watching?" Alicia asked, turning her attention back to the Ancient.

"Of course, I have, of course. Why would I not be watching you, my child? You know I sent my cougar to follow you. To take care of you."

"Yes, I know that *now*," she said. "Vulcan told me. But I think I scared Tawny off with my magic."

"And such magic it is!" he exclaimed. "The magic of the Ancients! Only better," he said in a quiet, mysterious tone, winking at her. "But look who is here!" The tall being turned and gestured at his home.

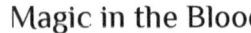

A Meeting with Destiny

From behind the sagging cabin stepped the golden cougar.

"Tawny!" Alicia cried and knelt down, beckoning the cat to her. "Tawny, come here. Oh please, come. *Pss, pss, pss.*" She made sounds as if calling a kitten. Extending her hand, she showed there was no fire hiding there, and she was not about to explode in flames.

The cat came slowly, cautiously at first, wary of the child. But when she saw there were no flames in the extended hand, her pace quickened almost to a trot, quickly reaching the girl and rubbing her cheek against Alicia's own. Alicia wrapped her arms around the fuzzy neck, hugging it as hard as she could.

"I love you, Tawny," the words spilled out of her. "I'm sorry I scared you. I didn't mean to. It was an impulse reaction. I was responding to the attack. It was out of my control. I'll learn to be better with my magic."

"And so, you shall, my child. And so, you shall," the Ancient said, looking down at the pair, human and cougar, still nestled snug.

Alicia craned her neck up at Thunderbolt from where she knelt. "I broke the barrier between worlds, and since then, I've seen strange things," she said. "But worse, I think I helped Gran'Tree get his power back."

"You did, oh yes you did," Thunderbolt replied. "Now we must set things right once more. I thought you were done. I thought you had fulfilled your destiny. But as it turns out, there is more left to do."

"What do you mean? What can I do?" she asked, pulling away from Tawny but still kneeling and scratching the cat on the head. "Can I fix the barrier?"

"What do I mean?" Thunderbolt repeated. "I mean, you need to use the power that was given to you by your parents. The power of thunder and fire combined. The power of the Ancients!

"The barrier is well and destroyed. There is no hope for that, none at all. Not now, anyway." He continued, speaking rapidly, not giving Alicia time to organize her thoughts. "But you have our magic, and you need to defeat Gran'Tree once and for all!"

"The power given to me by my parents?" Alicia asked, confused by this ongoing stream of words from the Ancient. She looked toward her dad. "The power of music? The power of song?"

"Uh, Thunderbolt?" Her father spoke up, a sense of urgency in his tone. "Um, I think we need to talk first. Privately. Now, before this conversation goes any further."

"Nonsense, she needs to know now." The old man shot an angry gaze toward Richard, before turning back to Alicia, all smiles. "There is no point in waiting, no point. I would prefer her mother to be here, but Gran'Tree is growing in strength again, and there is no time to wait!"

"But, uh . . ." her father began, before Alicia cut him off.

"My mother?" she asked, looking back at Thunderbolt. "She's not coming here; she stayed back at the cabin."

"Not *that* mother, child," Thunderbolt said. "Your *real, biological* mother. Vulcan!"

"What?" Alicia slowly rose to her feet, staring at Thunderbolt. "Vulcan?"

"Yes, of course!" the Ancient replied. "And I, my child, am your father."

 A Meeting with Destiny

FOURTEEN YEARS AGO

The young man rowed his small boat out across the glassy lake. He was heading for one of his favorite fishing spots, where the reeds grew tall from the calm water, not far from the shore of Moose Beach.

This was the man's almost nightly ritual. After dinner, he would grab his fishing pole and select a few choice flies, perhaps even taking a new one he had tied himself the night before. He had his favorite of course, which he always kept ready in his well-used, well-organized tackle box. He never knew what might interest the fish on any given evening. He enjoyed experimenting with a variety of flies, some sleek and narrow, like a fat mosquito, others round fluffy like a fuzzy bumblebee. The avid outdoorsman would take his gear and walk down the short trail to his dock, his young wife watching him leave from her spot at her canvas and easel, knowing that fishing brought him as much joy as painting gave her.

He was an expert fly-fisherman, learning the skill from his father-in-law, an excellent angler himself. But where the older man would drop his line in a spot a couple of times before moving on, the younger man had a patience not often seen in someone of his age. He knew that given enough time and enough casting, the large fish lurking deep in any particular hole, would not be able to resist the tantalizing bait.

He would cast out to let the fly dance on the surface of the water between the lily pads, imitating a real insect and creating the tiniest of ripples for just a moment before jerking the fishing pole back whip-like, the line arcing overhead, and casting out again, watching the fly sail forward to land in precisely the same spot.

Neighbors could see his silhouetted actions in the dying light of the day. They knew he would return when it got almost too dark to see with a basket full of rainbow trout which he often shared with them.

On this particular night, the man was feeling out of sorts. His wife was upset, and he did not know how he could fix things. He was a fixer by nature, but some problems did not have an easy solution.

His wife wanted a child. She had looked forward to being a mother for many years, even before marriage. But the news from the doctors wasn't good. In fact, given her desire, it was the worst news possible, and it seemed that having a child was not meant to be.

Because of this, the man's patience was not what it normally was, and he repeatedly tugged the fly back too quickly, not giving the fish that swam there a chance to take the bait. And so, his basket remained as empty as the nursery he and his wife had already started planning back home.

After an hour of this, he was ready to give up and head back to his cabin when off in the distance, he heard the faintest of noises. It sounded sort of like a fawn bleating or maybe an odd bird call, but one he did not recognize.

Listening intently, he heard it again. The sound was coming from the woods just beyond the shore of Moose Beach, which was nearby. Curiosity got the best of him, so the man rowed closer to the small strip of sand they called a beach, but in truth, it was barely a beach at all.

The soft evening wind shifted directions, bringing the sound to him as clear as a bell. He recognized it at once and felt a new urgency to find the source. It was the sound of a baby crying softly! But this side of the lake was wildly overgrown, and cabins had never been built in this area.

There were not even any nearby hiking trails or camping spots. How could a baby possibly be here?

He pulled on the oars with more energy and rowed the nose hard into shore, feeling the sand crunch below the bow of the yellow and green rowboat. Stepping out carefully, the man moved into the thick grasses just beyond the edge of the lake, searching.

The cry came once again, loudly this time. The young man turned toward it, moved past bushes that caught briefly on his pants and stopped. There, nestled into the soft grass, was the sweetest, cutest little girl he could imagine, naked as the day she was born.

The man knelt quickly, taking his jacket off and wrapping it

around the crying infant. He lifted the child carefully, cradling her small head, and looked around wildly, his eyes moving back and forth, scanning the woods.

"Hello! *HELLO!*" he called loudly, his voice echoing through the forest and across the lake. It only served to make the baby cry louder, even as the man gently rocked her. "Shh, shh, little one. It's ok. We'll find your mama," he comforted the child.

The baby soon calmed from the rocking and snuggled deeper into the man's jacket, which was still warm from his body heat. Frantic and desperate now, knowing the mother must be scared to death at losing her child, the man continued to call into the woods, but there was no response. *What to do, what to do?*

By now, the evening sky was quite dim, and the man decided the best solution would be to row home before it got dark and talk with his wife. They could contact the lodge and see if a child had been reported missing. He didn't know, but being a fixer, he was confident he would think of something.

The man picked his way through the bushes and returned to his boat. He climbed back in and rested the child on the floorboards, wrapped warmly in his down jacket. She was silent now and stared up at him with wide, clear eyes. Taking up his oars, the man braced them against the lakebed and pushed hard to free the boat from the sandy shore. Spinning the rowboat around, he headed for home, watching the woods behind Moose Beach slowly grow dark and distant.

Wait a second! What was that? It looked like a sort of shimmer in the air. Like he could see, not past the closest trees, but rather *through* them into a space beyond. A brighter and more colorful space. *And was that a statue of a woman? How was it possible he had*

A Meeting with Destiny

never seen this before?

The light continued fading, and the young man paused his rowing and blinked his eyes, squinting to see more clearly. Suddenly, everything looked as it always had. There was no shimmer. There was no statue. There was only darkness beyond the trees. And a small child resting on the floorboards of his rowboat.

Vulcan watched the man leave, and a tear rolled down her porcelain cheek. She had seen him before, more than once, as he fished in his favorite spots. He looked like a kind and patient man. A smart man. A gentle man. And she believed in her heart that her child could be raised safely by him. One day, when the child was ready, she would return to the Wild Side and, with her powers, end the threat that Vulcan and the other Ancients had created. Vulcan was sure of it. She had to be, to give up so much.

She watched until she could no longer see the man in the darkness, then turned sadly away and headed home to her hot springs, colorful twinkling lights flying through the air around her, accompanying her and lighting the way.

As she gave up so much.

The man and his wife never found the mother of that child. They spent days, weeks asking all around the lake. They put a notice up at the lodge. No child had been reported missing, no one had seen a family with a baby, and no one came forward to claim the little girl. They could not imagine where she had come from. Over time, their efforts to find the mother diminished.

By the time summer came to an end, the girl had become part of their family, and they were happy. They decided to care for her and love her as if she were their own child. And maybe she was, in some way. A gift from God at a time when it was needed the most.

They named the girl . . . Alicia.

9

TRUTH & LIES

Alicia's father finished telling his story with some help from Thunderbolt. It was out now. There was no more hiding what happened. He looked deflated, as if the weight of carrying, and now relieving himself of, this hidden truth had sapped all of his energy.

Alicia remained silent, trying to take in all she had heard. Without realizing it, she slowly backed away from her father and Thunderbolt, holding her hands forward waist high, palms out in a "wait, wait, hold on" gesture, her eyes darting between them. Her calves bumped against a fallen log at the edge of the clearing, and she sat down on it—hard. Sensing her emotions, Tawny padded over to the girl and sat on the ground beside her. Alicia looked at the cat, then to the ground for a moment, finally looking back up at the men standing before her.

Two fathers. One biological and one . . . well, one she had believed was undeniably her father, up until this moment at least. A feeling, dark and unpleasant, was rising in her.

No one noticed the sky turning grey above them. Storm clouds were slowly beginning to gather, blocking out the sun's rays that had warmed them all morning.

When she found her voice again, Alicia asked, "You said the power of thunder and fire combined. The power of the Ancients. Vulcan's *and* your powers?"

"Yes, yes, my child," Thunderbolt responded, still animated, not noticing the change coming over the girl. "My power and your mother's. But not drained as ours have been. Not weakened. No sir, yours are just being born!" He jogged in place, his grin widening so much, Alicia thought his face would split. It looked inhuman. She could practically see his back teeth. "Fresh and new. Fresh. And. New!"

The skies grew darker as Alicia's mind whirled with this new information. She thought hard before speaking. "So, I can summon fire, but I can also bring a storm?" Thunder rumbled softly in the distance.

"Of course you can! You can make it rain like nobody before you!"

Alicia looked down again as her thoughts swirled, returning to something she had heard before. Something that was told to her three years ago by a friend. A giant friend. A friend who succumbed to The Drying and was taken from her.

Bristleback, the mountain troll who helped her on her very first visit to this realm.

"There is strength and power in you that I have never seen in one so small," he had growled. *"Like lightning and fire behind your eyes."*

She had never forgotten those words, even when her parents had made her believe it was all a dream. Back then, the words had given her the strength to face off against Gran'Tree. In her own world, they had given her the courage to stand up to bullies.

If she had only known three years ago what they truly meant, what Bristleback had really seen within her, what she could really have done with her powers. Bringing rain, she might even have been able to save the troll from The Drying that took his life and turned him into dust.

The two men glanced skyward as light drops of precipitation began to patter against their heads. The grin on the Ancient's face grew obscene and clown-like with excitement as he stuck his dry, wrinkled tongue out to catch the falling water.

Alicia looked up again through hair that was glistening, wet strands dangling down in front of her eyes. "If I can create rain, I might have been able to save a friend," she said quietly, almost a whisper, simmering anger in her voice. Tawny raised her head to look at the girl upon hearing the tone.

"Yes, but you were not ready. Too young," the Ancient replied joyfully, looking back down at the girl. He was filled with anticipation for the storm looming above, proof of Alicia's power, but oblivious to the storm brewing inside his daughter. "Now you are old enough. So now you can know everything!"

Alicia stood. "I DO know everything . . . now!" she pronounced, clenching her fists tightly. The cat stood as well, taking steps to the side, the rain beginning to mat down her furry head. The smile slowly slipped from Thunderbolt's face. "And I understand that if I had known everything three years ago, I could have *saved* the life of a friend!"

Glaring sideways at her father, *her fake father*, she snarled, unclenching a fist and pointing an angry finger toward him. "And I know *you* lied to me!" she snarled. "For three years, you made me believe that my visit to the Wild Side wasn't real. But you knew. You *knew!* I can't believe you *KNEW!*" Alicia began to pace in circles as thunder boomed loudly overhead. "You'd seen the barrier yourself when you found me. You saw Vulcan! *No, it's all in your head. It's all make-believe*," she said mockingly, mimicking her father.

"Alicia . . . ," her father began.

"LIAR!" she screamed, spinning to face him. Now the dark skies opened up with a fury, and rain poured down on the group. She stabbed her finger at him again and again, emphasizing every word. "You. Are. A. LIAR! You *KNEW!*"

"Alicia, please," her father tried again.

"NO, I don't want to talk to you!" She returned to her pacing, soaking wet now but not caring. "You *knew,* and you *lied* to me, and *you*," she said, pointing at Thunderbolt, "you could have found me when I was here three years ago and told me what I had. What I *was.* What powers I could control." She stopped pacing again and faced the pair. "But you didn't! Neither of you told me the truth."

The two men stood quietly and accepted her anger, the smile now completely gone from the Ancient's face.

"But now I know what I have," she declared. "And I don't need either of you. Because I have power!" Lightning *cracked* across the sky as she spoke, causing Tawny to quickly move under the limbs of a nearby tree for cover.

Alicia spun with a determined stride, splashing water with each step. "DON'T follow me!" she yelled back at them as she fled the clearing and headed down the trail in the same direction that they had come.

Tawny looked at the two men standing still, watching the girl go. She hesitated for only a moment and then burst from under the tree and sprinted after Alicia.

Thunderbolt stood frozen in the downpour, his long grey hair dripping, watching Alicia and the cat leave. When they were out of sight, he looked to the man called Richard.

"*That* did not go as planned," he said. The Ancient then turned toward his cabin, leaving the human standing alone in the rain, entered his rickety home, and locked the door behind him.

Richard watched him leave, saw a thin trail of smoke beginning to ascend from the small stovepipe chimney, and wondered what had just happened. After a brief hesitation, he set about gathering his stuff. Alicia had left her things behind, but he couldn't carry them all. Against her wishes, Richard started after his daughter, hoping against hope that he could make things right again.

10

SORROW

Alicia wound her way down the mountain trail as quickly as she could, given the steep terrain. She wanted to get as far away from those two *men* as possible. She couldn't believe it! The lies, the deception. The father she knew had always told her, "One of the most important things in life is being honest. Even small lies can ruin the trust others place in you."

Well, this was no small lie. This was big, big. Maybe even the king of all lies. She could *maybe* understand not telling her about where she came from. How do you explain, "We found you in the woods?" But hiding knowledge of the Wild Side from her?

Alicia spent days arguing with her parents about what she had experienced. They always said she was making things up. Just the active imagination of an eleven-year-old, which would have made sense if they hadn't known about the Wild Side. But clearly, her dad had seen *something*. Even that little bit, that tiniest glimpse across the barrier, should have had him saying, *you know what? I saw something once that I can't explain, so I don't completely doubt you.*

But no, they had made it out like *she* was the liar. Like *she* was just making things up to get attention or to have an excuse for hiding from her dad. But it had really happened, and they knew it, and now she knew that they knew it!

Now that she had knowledge of the power that Thunderbolt had given her, Alicia thought back. The signs were there, but she hadn't seen them or even thought to look!

I've known you for a very long time. You did what you were born to do.

 Sorrow

Thunderbolt had spoken those words to her during their first meeting just a few weeks ago. Vulcan had said the same thing, but Alicia's anger had driven her to leave before she learned what she was born to do.

"And here I am doing the same thing again. Running away. How stupid am I?" The girl said to no one as she raced down the mountain.

The rain continued to pour relentlessly out of the sky, creating streams of water that ran down the trail ahead of her and made the descent slippery. Flashes of lightning brightened the murky forest in sporadic bursts as thunder rolled over the treetops. Alicia was drenched and needed to keep wiping the rain from her eyes, but she didn't care. She had to get away as quickly as possible, put some distance between her and those two liars.

She was shivering and cold now and suddenly realized she had left everything behind. Her pack, her jacket, her sleeping bag, her food. She stopped and looked back, considering for half a second returning to get her stuff. And there was Tawny, following not far behind, her golden coat looking shaggy and wet.

Alicia smiled briefly at the sight and waited for Tawny to catch up. She was not angry with the cat. Tawny was there for her. Now, her only friend and her only support. She felt bad for scaring her earlier.

"Hi, girl," she said when the cat reached her. "I guess it's just you and me. I'm not going back there. I don't need my stuff. I've got you." She continued to shake from the cold as she stroked the wet fur on the soaked cat's head. "Let's go. Let's get off this stupid mountain."

They continued down the muddy path. Alicia didn't have a direction in mind yet. She just wanted to get back to the lake and leave her two fathers behind.

Alicia stepped carefully out onto the fallen tree, glancing down into the canyon, unable to see the bottom. The rain had not stopped, and the tree bridge was shiny with pools of water collecting in the small cracks in the bark. Even though the tree trunk was plenty wide enough, the curved surface could be slippery, which made her uneasy. That, combined with the shivering in her body, took away some of the confidence, so she would need to progress slowly to the other side.

Tawny watched from behind, eyes riveted on the girl like a mother watching her own child. After all they had been through, the cat considered this human to be her family and would do anything to protect her.

Alicia lowered herself to her hands and knees again. There was no other option, and she began to make her way across the log. It wasn't too difficult, just slow, and her knees hurt every time they would land in her wet pants on a knobby bit of tree. But she was being careful to place each hand and knee securely before moving forward.

The rain was blinding her vision, and Alicia paused to shake the hair from her face. She used the back of her hand that wasn't dirty from the tree bark to wipe the rain from her eyes and looked forward. "Almost halfway across now," she told herself, tired of being out in the open in this storm.

She continued moving forward, but her left shoe snagged on a branch. Alicia turned back to look, tugging gently so she wouldn't slip, and watched as the branch moved, bent, and wrapped around her ankle.

A realization dawned on her! Gran'Tree must have sent a root digging *through* the fallen tree from the far end! And now she was trapped, more roots emerging to circle her leg.

Alicia rose quickly up onto her knees and snapped her wet fingers hard. Nothing happened. There was no flame. She snapped her fingers again, and a small spark, barely visible, crackled there but was quickly extinguished by the rain. "Ohhh, no!" She snapped them again and again, but her fingers were becoming numb as roots continued to burst from the tree behind her, snaking around both legs now, binding her tightly to the bridge.

She didn't stop. Alicia snapped and snapped, repeatedly trying to draw the fire magic forth, but with no success. Panicking, she looked around for something she could use to smash the roots entangling her legs. But what? She was on a fallen tree far from land. There was nothing!

She heard a growl and saw movement through the falling rain. Suddenly Tawny was there behind her, slashing with her razor-sharp claws! They tore through the roots as if made of wax, slicing through her pants as well and nicking her skin, stinging, and drawing thin lines of blood. Alicia didn't care about the pain. That sweet cat was going to save her!

Chunks of the roots fell away, and what remained quickly withdrew into the tree, disappearing from view. Alicia guessed they did not want to tangle with a mother cat when her "kitten" was being threatened. Alicia's legs were free!

She dropped to all fours again, placing her hands back on the trunk, and began scrambling forward, more quickly this time, in case the roots came back. Tawny followed closely behind, prepared for another attack.

What neither of them noticed was that the combination of the heavy rain and the quick, fierce encounter with the roots had caused a large patch of soggy moss growing on the old tree bridge to come loose.

As she passed, Tawny unknowingly placed a back paw on that patch of loosened moss. It held for a moment, trying to maintain its weakened grip on the tree. And then the moss tore off.

Alicia heard a frightened yowl and looked over her shoulder, shaking the rain from her eyes again. What she saw sent chills racing through her body, freezing her even more than the storm already had.

Tawny was hanging from the side of the fallen tree by her front paws, claws dug into the wet wood. Her back right paw was clinging desperately to a downward facing branch, and her left was scrabbling for purchase on the underside of the tree and failing.

"Tawny, no!" Alicia turned her body as quickly as possible and crawled back to the struggling cat. Flattening herself against the tree bridge, she grabbed Tawny's front paw and pulled. "Come on, I've got you!"

The cat's left paw continued to scratch against the bottom of the tree, scraping free bits of old, wet bark and sending it falling in pieces into the roar from below. After several attempts, Tawny's paw found a tiny crack in the wood, and her nails stuck, holding her in place. Relief and determination replaced the panic on the cat's face, and Alicia redoubled her efforts.

"We've got this," she said encouragingly to Tawny, digging deep to find her strength while tugging on the paw.

 Sorrow

Suddenly, the thin branch that had been supporting Tawny's right paw snapped.

With that support gone, her back left paw could no longer maintain its hold on the crack, and it also slipped free with a shower of bark. Now all the cat's massive weight was being held by her front paws as she dangled from the side of the bridge with the young girl holding tightly to Tawny's wet and slippery foot.

Alicia pulled with all her might, but the huge cat was far too heavy and began to slide, dragging the girl with her along the slippery bridge and toward the edge.

Alicia's body began to hang over the side and now she could see beyond the edge of the log bridge and past the cat to the treetops and darkness below them. "Try and climb, Tawny! Try!" she cried. "I can't hold on! I can't." The cat's sharp nails tore deep furrows through the wood, and her wet paw slipped slowly and inevitably through Alicia's hands and down the side of the tree.

"I can't hold on!" Alicia cried again, her fingers trying hopelessly to lock around the huge paw. But it wasn't enough.

The last of her claw hold gave way, and Tawny, the golden cougar, fell backward past the tips of pine trees and into the rain, mist, and darkness, disappearing from sight into the canyon below.

Alicia watched wide-eyed at where the cat disappeared and gave a hiccupping cough. Then a wailing cry rose from her throat. She stood and spun back toward land, moving more quickly than was safe to finish the crossing and reach the far ledge. Leaping off the end of the tree bridge, she climbed up from the small ledge to more solid ground, looked to her right, and sprinted off into the woods, following the edge of the canyon, searching desperately for any path down to the bottom.

In her rush, Alicia did not see that her father, Richard, had reached the far side of the tree bridge behind her. He heard a scream through the storm's noise and rushed forward, stopping at the canyon's edge to look down and across. Richard saw no sign of his daughter. Fearing the worst, he stepped out onto the natural bridge.

Alicia ran headlong between the trees. There was no trail to follow here, and she crashed through branches and bushes that reached out with wet limbs, trying to slow her and trip her up.

The mountain began to slope downwards, and she slipped on wet patches of pine needles and debris, going down hard repeatedly, scraping skin from her forearms and elbows. But each time, she pushed herself to her feet, ignoring the stinging pain, and continued her race downhill.

Alicia didn't know how far she had run. It could have been a mile, maybe more, maybe less. But before long, even through the steady thrum of pounding rain, she could finally hear the roar of crashing water becoming louder and louder. The canyon river was close.

At last, she emerged from the woods into an open area, finding a small deer trail that carved its way down the hillside to her right and disappeared over the cliff's edge. She maneuvered along the narrow trail, picking her way carefully now that she was so close, and found a steep path down the side of the cliff to a mass of boulders below.

Shuffling down this steeper slope, Alicia reached the bottom and stepped out onto an enormous, flat rock the size of a small car.

 *Sorrow*

She stopped, her breath coming in huge heaving gasps, and looked over the edge, where she could see the river raging, so close she could almost touch it.

It appeared swollen even more than normal due to the torrential downpour, and the sound here was almost deafening, echoing and re-echoing around the steep walls as the water pounded the polished sides of the canyon. Gigantic rocks, jagged and dangerous, rose sharply from the water as far as she could see, like the broken teeth of some massive serpent. The river sent huge sprays up into the air as it navigated its unstoppable course down the mountain.

All hope died in Alicia, as surely as Tawny, her beloved and only remaining companion, died here. Nothing could have survived that fall. Nothing.

Alicia sat down on the big stone, exhausted. The rain continued to fall unabated around her. Soaking wet and shivering, she pulled her knees to her chest, wrapped her arms around them, and sobbed uncontrollably.

11

WISDOM FROM BOB

An hour or more passed before the rain tapered off and eventually stopped. Alicia, emptied and chilled, slowly unfolded herself and stood. Her body ached as if she had been punched repeatedly, and her arms stung viciously from multiple abrasions she had collected in her race down the mountain.

She felt the loss of the beloved cat intensely. The cat she had adored and who she knew felt the same. Her chest ached. Alicia wept until there was nothing left to come out, and then she cried some more.

Sneezing once, then again, and then a third time before looking around, Alicia's world was saturated with water, and she was lost. Not completely, she knew the general direction of the lake, but she was in a place she had never been and had no companions to help guide her.

The feeling of being lost was not just physical. Alicia was lost emotionally as well, drained down to her very core. Her family, as she had known it, had been destroyed. She had powers stronger than she ever imagined, but the ability to actually save her friends was still beyond her control. And those powers could do nothing to remove this overwhelming feeling of hopelessness.

Alicia was angry, too. Furious. She had a murderous tree that was killing animals and hunting her. She had been lied to by those most important to her. And now Tawny, a trusted companion, died while saving her. All because of this stupid, stupid Wild Side. She wished desperately that life could return to what it was before. That

she could forget ever stumbling into this place.

Alicia sneezed again, rubbed her nose, and thought—everything, *everything* led back to one being—Gran'Tree. He was hunting her now, and she had been lucky to escape twice. He was part of the reason her parents . . . *Parents*, she scoffed . . . he was the reason *they* got trapped, and she had to break the barrier. Evidently, he was even the reason she had been born at all. Defeating him was what she had been born to do, according to Thunderbolt.

But worst of all, Gran'Tree was the reason Tawny was now dead.

Alicia hated that tree. Hated it with all her being. She was going to destroy Gran'Tree! She would burn him to the ground with her magic. And God help anyone who got in her way! She would burn the world if she had to. After all, that's all she was, right? Just a tool created for destruction. A weapon that could be wielded as easily and as dangerously as a gun. She didn't care. Everyone was a liar anyway. Alicia had no one. She would fulfill her dumb destiny. She would burn it all.

Flames rose unbidden in her hand. She felt a tingle and looked down, surprised but willing them to grow larger. The flames licked up her arm, across her shoulders, and fell in a blanket down her body, like putting on a summer dress. Alicia was magic. She was *fire!* And she would have her revenge.

Feeling the enormity of the power within her, Alicia drew harder on the magic. The sensation of pins and needles prickled across her body, like after having a foot fall asleep. She sensed the awakening of a new sort of muscle and let the flames rise up, raging now and burning bright. They dried her clothes and hair. They flickered high above, crackling and heating the surrounding air.

Alicia continued to let the flames burn for a moment, then made a fist, sending the flames traveling back up her body until they disappeared. She could feel her body sag as the magic left, its use taxing her energy. But Alicia was gaining control. She could feel it. And she would use it.

Alicia stepped away from the large rock, leaving behind a smoldering boulder and the river that had stolen away her friend and protector.

It was late afternoon, the sun heating the day again and removing all signs of the impromptu thunderstorm. Alicia felt miserable.

Shortly after stepping off the rock, walking back up the small trail and into the forest, she realized she was once again at risk of attack from the roots of Gran'Tree. Pausing in her journey, Alicia snapped her fingers and watched the fire in her hand. Focusing, she willed the flames to expand, slowly and softly. No more than a candle flame, really. She imagined opening a faucet just a tiny bit so only a trickle of water flowed, but in this case, it was magic. She felt it as a tingle and Alicia guided the flow across her hand, sheathing it like a glove. With her mind, she opened the tap a bit more, a bit more, there! The young witch could sense the magic go from barely more than a quick drip drip drip, tickling her blood stream, to a steady current, like a sugar rush.

The flames grew brighter for a moment, and now she allowed the stream to flow down her arm and once again shroud her in its warmth. The fire dimmed as it covered her, wrapping her body from head to toe. Alicia had stopped opening the mental tap and left the magic running just like that. Now she was bathed in soft light, sort of like wearing armor. It was barely visible. Just a warm glow and heat shimmering in the air above her skin, like she might see rising above an asphalt road on a hot day.

Alicia felt protected from the roots now, but the armor of flames had not relieved the bitter cold that was set so deep in her bones not even the sun could chase it away. The exertion of the hike, the rain, the deep sorrow of her loss, and now the steady drain of magic all sapped her strength and were taking their toll on her young body.

Beginning her trek again, Alicia was shivering and hungry. She had not eaten anything since the breakfast bars in the morning. Searching as she hiked, she found a large patch of huckleberry bushes. Reaching the edge of the patch, she crouched looking beneath the leaves for berries.

The branches and leaves were still wet from the rain, but the water sizzled as it touched her, evaporating immediately. Alicia stretched her hand out and slowly reached to pluck a small berry. The weak flame surrounded the berry, but it did not burn. It was as if, on a subconscious level, the magic was tuned to her wants or needs and adapted when necessary. Like when the roots were attacking everyone, she had touched her dad's shoulder, and the flames rushed across him, burning away the roots but leaving him uninjured. The same thing had happened with Tawny.

Her magic *knew* what she wanted, even without directly thinking about it! This was a new discovery, but her understanding and use of it did not feel precise yet. She was still learning. The fire had burned the ground, even scorching the rock she stood on before and the water from the bushes as well. But when she thought about wanting the berry, it remained unharmed.

Alicia looked at the trail she had left behind her, searching for her footsteps. There were no charred patches visible, her subconscious understanding the potential danger of burning the forest floor.

Alicia would need to practice more to fully grasp her capabilities. She was pretty sure she had summoned the storm, like one hundred percent sure, which came without her calling it. The weather had reacted to her growing rage. She wondered if that might be a good thing, a sort of self-defense mechanism that responded to her emotions. She could not control it yet, but she had been furious when it began.

And now her hatred was directed at the great yellow pine. He would see the power she had now, and he would cower before her.

Returning her attention to the huckleberries, she dug into the bushes for more of the goodies, and found a few, savoring each one slowly. Yes, she was very hungry but did not know when she might find food again. Alicia did not even have a knife with her that she could use to sharpen a spear for fishing. On top of that, her stomach was not feeling so well, so she ate delicately, one berry at a time, enjoying each one individually.

As she picked between the leaves, Alicia became aware of a heavy shuffling *sshl-OP*, *sshl-OP* noise moving through the bushes. It came from somewhere off to her right, but in her crouched position, it was hard to see above the brush. Some creature was moving over there. She could smell its fur now, recently drenched from the rain and heavy with musk, like a wet dog. Alicia stayed down, just wanting the thing to go away. She was in a foul mood and did not want to be bothered.

She wished Tawny were here. The cat would chase away the intruder, leaving her in peace to finish her meal. But Tawny wasn't here, and the shuffling grew closer.

Finally, standing up irritated, Alicia shouted, "Shoo. Go awa . . . oh!"

There, just a few yards away, was a large black bear, moving through the huckleberry bushes, searching for his own meal of berries beneath the small leaves. Alicia saw the longish cream-colored nose and the rounded ears, now swiveled in her direction. And she saw the brown, close-set eyes looking her way.

"I will not shoo," the bear said in a low, gruff voice. "I will not go away. This is my berry patch." The bear turned his eyes from her direction and continued his quest for huckleberries, paying the girl no mind.

"Oh!" she said again. "You can talk!" The bear was big, maybe three times the size of a Saint Bernard. Its black fur was short and lay flat across its broad back. The legs were like small tree trunks.

"So can you," he replied, sounding bored. He grabbed a branch with his great paw and held it in place, using his tongue and lips to pull some of the tangy, purple berries from the plant.

"Yes, but . . . you're an animal," Alicia said, stunned that after all this time, she had found another of the denizens of the Wild Side that could speak. She had not encountered one since she was eleven and lost here in this realm, looking for a way to get back home.

The bear stopped his search and stared at Alicia again like he was annoyed at having to explain things to her.

"Let us be clear," he said. "You are an animal too. Just because you can walk around on two legs does not make you any better than me." He spoke to her slowly as if he believed her to be a fool. The bear went back to searching for berries. "And I should tell you that you are on fire."

Alicia ignored this second part and considered for a moment. "Yes, but I'm human. And I have magic."

"I know who you are, and I know what you have," the bear said. "Everyone knows. You are becoming famous in these parts. The Burning Girl, they call you. But *that* does not make you any better than me, either."

"I didn't say it did," she said defensively. "I was just surprised, is all. It's been years since I spoke to an anim . . ." She almost said "animal." "Since I spoke to another being of this realm that didn't look human." She paused. "And Gran'Tree, I guess," she added.

She thought about the other voices she had heard while hiking to Thunderbolt. Could those have been creatures as well? Maybe with the magic returned, she could talk to them all again.

"You know, he is back," The bear said. "Whatever the legends say you did, you did not defeat him. Hurt him, maybe, but that is all. And made him angry too." The bear stuck his snout into a nearby bush and slurped up a few berries.

"Yeah, I know. He attacked me," Alicia said. "And he killed my friend. Not directly, but he caused it to happen. I hate him so much!" she spat the last words.

"Hate. Not a good word. Not a good feeling. Not a good thing." The bear looked at her again and stopped his search, plopping his ample behind on the ground. "Gran'Tree has hate. I believe he hates you for what you did to him four thousand years ago."

Alicia looked surprised by this comment, her mouth forming

a small "o." "Yes, everyone knows the legend of the girl who sang and saved the lands, withering the great tree in the process," he continued. "And now his hatred is controlling him and making him worse than he ever was before."

"I don't care," she said loudly, brows furrowing and color rising in her cheeks. The flames surrounding her flared briefly like the sun. "He's had a part in destroying everything I've loved. He can die for all I care. I hate him, and he deserves to die." She looked down, her voice getting quiet. "I will get revenge for what he's done to me. That's all I'm good for anyway."

"That may be true," the bear replied. "Partially," he added. "Gran'Tree may need to be defeated once and for all. But watch yourself, girl," he warned. "Hate could destroy you in the process."

"Do you want to travel with me?" Alicia asked, her voice rising with optimism. She missed Tawny, and she didn't want to be alone anymore. The bear might be kind of grumpy, but oddly enough, she sorta liked him.

"No," the black bear replied. "I do not much care for humans. And I do not much care for magic either. If you have not noticed, you fit both those categories. This is your crusade, and I will leave you to it."

With that said, the bear stood, turned, and wandered off in a different direction, pine needles crunching underfoot with each step, *sshl-OP, sshl-OP*. Alicia watched him go. "Hey," she called out. "Be careful if you see any wriggling roots!"

"Oh, he does not bother me," the bear called back over his shoulder. "Not yet anyway. Maybe I am just too big. For now, at least." The bear continued walking away. "In a month or two, who knows?" *sshl-OP, sshl-OP* "He may just eat the whole world."

Alicia shuddered at the thought. She began to go her own way but stopped, turning back toward the bear. "Hey, what's your name?"

"Bob. My name is Bob."

And with that, the big bear's hindquarters were swallowed up by the bushes.

Alicia gathered a few more berries and turned south, heading in the general direction of the lake. She decided she really did like Bob. She liked him very much.

12

JELLIES OF THE LAKE

As afternoon turned into evening and the empty spaces between the trees once again filled with black shadows, Alicia finally reached the bottom of the mountain. She wasn't far from the lakeshore now, and her magical fire armor . . . she thought about that for a moment. *Magical fire armor. Cool.* Her magical fire armor cast a soft glow about her that lit the path. But the constant drain of the magic was making her a bit light-headed.

Different sorts of noises came with the night. The bird calls of robins and jays and the annoyed chattering of squirrels were replaced by the hoot of a great horned owl in a distant tree and the feathery fluttering of bat wings as they swooped around her, gobbling up the insects that were attracted to the light emanating from Alicia.

She decided to continue thinking of Richard as her dad despite learning the truth, and wondered briefly what he and Thunderbolt were doing, but realized she didn't much care. Alicia was still furious with both of them and her mother, Kate, too, even though *she* had never seen evidence of the Wild Side. Her mother had known Alicia was not hers and never said anything. But Alicia thought again, *what would my mother have said?* and decided that, perhaps, she was being unfair. Realizing the need to redirect her anger, she changed her focus to Gran'Tree.

Alicia considered what Bob the bear had said. Was she overreacting with her feelings? No, she told herself. She had every reason to hate the big tree. She could control the hate she was feeling. She knew that. *Aim it at Gran'Tree*, she thought. *Take him down!*

As she made her own path through the woods heading for the lake to see if there was any chance of catching a fish, the still of the evening brought hushed whispers to her again. Alicia found that if she focused her listening the same way that she had focused on controlling the fire, she could tune out the static and hear words more clearly.

"That's Alicia!"

"She's 'The Burning Girl.'"

The Burning Girl, Alicia thought. *That is what they are calling me? Bob called me that, too.*

"Legends say she fought Gran'Tree before," the voices continued.

"Your great, great, great, a hundred-times-great-grandfather knew her!"

Could that be a descendant of Mickey? she thought. *Tucked away in a burrow somewhere close? Watching her through the pine needles that hid its doorway? Or maybe a far distant grandchild of Briar the jay!*

"Come out," Alicia said softly, stopping in her tracks. "I won't hurt you. Come out, please!" She was incredibly lonely and sad and felt a desperate need for company for any distraction from her thoughts.

But the woods were silent. There was no response. Alicia had grown bigger and taller in the years since her first visit and was bathed in magic. It must be too frightening for the smaller creatures to approach.

Alicia sneezed and pushed onward, continuing her journey to who knew where. The voices returned, but she tuned them out. They made her unhappy. She kicked out at a loose stone and watched it go sailing through the air to land and tumble off into some brush a short distance away. Alicia did not mean to scare the creatures. But mostly she was sad because they brought back memories of her friends from long ago. She felt so alone, like she had lost everybody close to her. Her friends and family were dead, gone, or she couldn't trust them. She thought she had no more tears left in her, but she was wrong.

The Burning Girl cried hot tears and trudged on through the flame-lit night.

The moon had not yet risen and in the black sky above, the stars were brilliant. The sky was awash with constellations as Alicia stepped out from the trees and onto the lake's shoreline. This was her favorite view in the whole world. The lake in front of her was wide and like glass. Not a single breeze disturbed the surface and the billions of stars shining down from above created dots of light on the water.

From here, Alicia could see the red star. Not really a star at all, but the planet Mars, twinkling gently. And if she looked closely, she could see the Milky Way galaxy splashed across the sky and reflected on the mirrored surface of the black lake, as if there were a multitude of stars in the darkness below as well.

She thought about space, the constellations, and the true wonder of nature. It was all so vast it made her head spin, so she sat down on the grassy shore, staring across the lake toward where her cabin stood on the opposite side. If she squinted, she could just make out a light coming from there. The porch light, perhaps, left on overnight to ward off the darkness and maybe to guide her home.

Was her mother worried about her? Did her father go home,

 Jellies of the Lake

or was he searching for her even now? She was too emotionally exhausted to remain mad at them. She would face that later after she dealt with Gran'Tree. *That* anger remained strong in her chest.

Looking across the water, Alicia saw faint ripples forming on the surface, along with a sort of sparkling she had never seen before, yet there was still no wind. As she watched, the disturbance grew stronger. When she stood, Alicia swayed a moment before regaining her balance. Something unseen was definitely causing a commotion beneath the glassy surface.

Lights were twinkling in the water now, not cast by the stars but coming from underneath, from the darkness below. She detected movement in those lights. A thrust up, then a slow drift down. Another thrust. Another slow drift.

Alicia raised her hand, casting her own light across the dark water. She was shocked and amazed at what she saw there. Hundreds of small jellyfish! Thousands! Translucent yellow creatures, each no bigger than the size of a golf ball, were flapping their umbrella-like hoods, driving up from the deep and sinking back down again. And they were alive with bioluminescent light!

Alicia had never seen such a thing. In fourteen summers of coming to the lake, she had no idea they even existed! But here they were, flocking to the magical light she cast, drawn to her like insects. Alicia giggled in awe at the sight.

The jellyfish formed a wide swath on the surface of the lake, like a goopy carpet of gel laid out before her. Flapping, swerving, undulating, they all seemed to be jostling for position to be closest to her, but there were just too many of them. The ones behind were pushing those in front up against the grassy shore.

Alicia watched in fascination and began to laugh with joy. She wanted to reach out and touch them, to step into the water and be surrounded by them. For some reason, she was drawn to this colony of creatures that were equally drawn to her. But she feared they may sting and drag her down into the black depths, and so remained on the shore, smiling and laughing. Such a sight to behold!

Alicia's magic swelled as she laughed, and her flames grew brighter, working the jellyfish into a frenzied flapping. The magic sapped her strength, but she could not control it. Laughter had taken over and suddenly, she felt very weak. Chills she had felt throughout the day now rushed through her limbs, causing her to shiver uncontrollably. Conversely, she felt a wave of heat sweep across her forehead, and tiny droplets of sweat burst forth.

Alicia collapsed to the ground, and the flames surrounding her extinguished. The last thing she remembered before losing consciousness were colorful lights in the trees, dancing and sweeping toward her.

And then, blackness.

13

THE RUMBLING SLUMBERER

She dreamed.

In her dream, Alicia rose into the air and floated through the woods. Small lights surrounded her in all directions. Colorful lights. Bright sun-like yellows and dazzling reds. Blues that sparkled like gemstones and green the color of lime popsicles.

The lights carried her on gossamer wings, flying above the bushes, between tree branches that reached out and lightly snagged her hair as she went past, leaving small strands hanging from the branches. In the distance, she heard music. A high four-note tune. Alicia was sure she had heard it before, beautiful beyond words. It was familiar, but she could not quite remember why. It called to her, called to the lights. The tune was summoning them. But to where she didn't know.

She was so tired, and this was such a pleasant dream. Alicia laid her head down, caught by the many lights that surrounded her, closed her eyes, and floated.

Alicia did not know how long she slept, but she woke in almost total darkness on a bed of grass. Shivering, she blinked, trying to clear the blurry vision and chase away the gloom. A figure approached. A woman, Alicia saw now, dressed in white from head to toe, almost translucent.

"Mom?" she asked.

The Rumbling Slumberer

"Go to sleep, my child. You are ill with fever."

"But where am I? Gran'Tree . . ." Her words echoed faintly back to her from the blackness. And beyond the edge of darkness, she was aware of a low grinding noise, repetitive and deep, like large stones sliding against one another.

"You are safe," the woman said gently. "Gran'Tree cannot reach you here. Go to sleep and rest."

Alicia closed her eyes again, exhausted, lulled back to sleep by the odd grinding noise. The sound . . . almost as if . . . the very earth itself was breathing.

Alicia was awakened sometime later by the rough grating of wood scraping on stone nearby. She opened her eyes, rubbed away the sleep, and lay there for a moment, smelling the grass of her bed and the musty air beyond.

Blinking, Alicia raised herself to her elbows and looked toward the sound she had heard. The woman she had seen earlier was standing beside her bed and two carved wooden bowls had been placed next to the groggy girl, one filled with some type of liquid, the other with berries and pine nuts.

Alicia rubbed her sleep-swollen eyes again, still hearing the rumble around her, and looked up at the woman. Only this time, she saw clearly. Not dressed in white, as she had previously thought. Her body itself was white. It was Vulcan, the Ancient.

"Ancient" certainly didn't describe the being before her. She may have been thousands of years old, but she looked to be in her thirties, beautiful and nude. Her entire body was as smooth as a polished stone, from her cascading hair, the color of milk, to her perfectly shaped toes. She was like a sculpted ivory statue come to life. Except for the eyes. Vulcan's eyes were a light blue, almost verging on grey, the color of the sky in Spring.

Alicia was not embarrassed by the nudity, as she had been the first time they met, even though there was nothing to see. She was still very tired, and the Ancient was no longer a stranger to her. In fact, the realization washed over her.

Vulcan was her mother.

"I see the recognition in your eyes, my child. The understanding. Yes, you are my daughter."

Alicia had, of course, already been told this, but seeing Vulcan here, now, made it seem more real than it felt when it was just a story told by her father.

"How long have I been here?" she asked. Her mouth was dry, and her throat sore. She could barely speak above a whisper.

"You have been asleep for almost two days now," Vulcan said. "Before that, I had my sprites watching you, though they remained hidden. I could sense the rage in you through them and knew you needed time to understand. But when I saw you collapse, I could wait no longer. You were in danger without your magic, so I had them bring you to me."

Two days, Alicia thought. Her parents must be worried now. *Not that I care,* she thought, but was forced to admit to herself that she *did* care. A little bit, anyway.

Looking at Vulcan, still trying to shake off the last remnants of sleep, Alicia asked, "When I was here before, why didn't you say anything? I was searching for answers, and you gave me nothing but cryptic words."

"I tried," Vulcan replied. "I wanted to tell you everything. You had returned, and I wanted to explain and welcome you back home. My daughter—returned! But you fled my springs before I could."

Alicia remembered that Vulcan had said something the first time they met. *We gave you the magic you needed to defeat Gran'Tree, Thunderbolt and I.* The Ancient had been trying to tell her! She had been so confused and frustrated; she just wasn't hearing it.

"But you let me go," Alicia said, eyes pleading with the Ancient for answers, asking her why, pain in her voice. "You let me go twice."

"You are right. I did. I had to, both times," Vulcan said in response. "You needed to find your way to become who you are now." She looked gently at Alicia. "My word, you were such a beautiful little child. And now, you are a beautiful and powerful young woman."

"I don't feel powerful right now," Alicia confessed. "But you haven't answered. Why did you let me go?"

"Here, I have brought water and food to help you regain your strength. Please, eat. And I will tell you everything."

Alicia sat up fully and looked around. The room they were in was mostly dark, but she got the sense, perhaps due to the slight echo, of a large, empty space. There were dim lights nearby, the flying colors from before, the Ancient's sprites. So, it hadn't been a dream after all. The sprites had carried her here.

Alicia remembered seeing the sprites when she first visited Vulcan at the hot springs that bore the Ancient's name a few weeks ago. They were Vulcan's window into the forest. She could see through the sprites' eyes as they traveled through the woods and she summoned

them back to her with a simple, haunting four-note tune.

The sprites, dozens, perhaps hundreds of them, were pocket-sized, humanoid beings with thin transparent wings. Their bodies glowed with a variety of assorted colors, some a teal green like a peacock's feathers, others a darker burnt orange like the sun sinking into the ocean. All the colors of the rainbow and more were there in their twinkling lights.

Alicia could see from the light of the glowing sprites that they were in a cave of some sort. The air smelled stale, and they were surrounded by walls made of grey rock. That must be the reason they were safe from Gran'Tree here. His questing roots could not penetrate the solid stone that encased them.

Alicia reached down and picked up the bowl of water. She was so thirsty, but the water was icy cold, so she sipped slowly, feeling it cool and soothe her throat as she swallowed while at the same time making her teeth ache.

Setting the water aside, she picked up the bowl of berries and nuts, slid herself so that her back was against the rough wall, and looked at Vulcan expectantly.

"Ok, as you wish." Vulcan took a breath and began. "Long ago, over fourteen years your time, but much, much longer for us, we Ancients saw what was happening to this land. We had created a monster in Gran'Tree."

"Yes," Alicia interrupted, speaking around a mouthful of food. "Thunderbolt told me the story of how you created the great tree accidentally when the three of you were creating the barrier."

"So, you already know part of the story. That is good. Now let me tell you the rest." Vulcan continued, sitting down across from Alicia.

"As I said, we saw what we had created. But at the same time, we were powerless to stop it." Vulcan gestured, her hands moving apart as she talked. "We had burned through our power, creating the barrier to forever cut off humans from the world of magic. We were tired and went our separate ways. And so, Gran'Tree grew unhindered." She tapped an index finger to the side of her head.

"*I* had an idea. We had little magic between us, but could we *create* magic? *New* magic! Would that be possible?" The Ancient was excited now. She sat taller and took a deep breath before continuing. "I left my home at the hot springs and set out to meet with Thunderbolt. I wanted nothing more to do with that troll, The Silver King, but I thought maybe, with Thunderbolt and my powers combined, we might be able to create something that had a chance."

Vulcan stood. "Thunderbolt was doubtful but willing to listen." She began pacing, hands in a constant state of motion, gesturing the grandness of her plan. "I persisted, convincing him of the potential. It could really work! A being with the powers of thunder and fire combined! I stayed there with him, that old, grumpy, beautiful man. And in the end, you were born. The most amazing and precious thing in the world!"

"If I was so amazing and precious, why did you send me away?" Alicia countered. "Why did you abandon me on the shore of the lake for someone to find? Was I only created to be a weapon and nothing more?"

"Ah, see my child, that is where it gets . . . complicated." Vulcan knelt in front of Alicia and looked directly into her eyes. "The truth is, we have no *love* in the Wild Side. That is an emotion reserved for humankind and the other creatures of your realm. When we created the barrier, it was out of anger and distrust at what humans were doing to the land. Those emotions were channeled into the magic, leaving behind a realm where love could not thrive. We closed ourselves off forever from that feeling." Vulcan looked sad at this revelation. "But you, you could have love. You could learn it, grow it, and nurture it in your soul. And that love could make you so very, very powerful. With that and our magic, you would have the strength to defeat Gran'Tree."

"It still sounds like I was only an instrument to be discarded. A tool. Are you saying you didn't love me?" Alicia asked, not wanting to hear the answer.

Vulcan returned to her seat, facing her daughter. "It is not that I do not love you. I am very fond of you, my child. You are so precious, so much more than just a tool. I care for you deeply . . . I truly do. It is that I *cannot* love you. I lack the ability to feel that emotion."

Alicia had no response to this. She looked down, eating her food without responding, a solitary tear rolling down her cheek.

Discovering that a parent didn't love her, even a parent she never knew she had, hurt more than she wanted to admit right now. Alicia wiped the tear away quickly with the back of her hand and looked up.

"Can you teach me how to control the magic?" she asked, choking back her emotions and changing the subject.

"I cannot do that either, child, not fully. I do not even know myself what you are truly capable of. I can only keep you safe. At least as much as my abilities will allow. And my sprites, of course." Vulcan stood up. "I can also provide guidance. And I can introduce you to an enormously powerful ally. Are you ready?"

Alicia sipped the rest of the water, finished the last of her berries and nuts, and nodded.

"Then come with me."

The Ancient reached out her hand. Alicia rose, lightheaded, and took the porcelain hand. With the glow of the sprites leading the way, they ventured deeper into the cave, following a smooth trail that led through a narrow gap between large rocks. Emerging from the other side, the sprites spread out, and Alicia could see an enormous cavern before her. It was absolutely immense. A whole stadium could fit in here! Or a plane or a blimp! And the ceiling was so high that the entire Statue of Liberty could have fit in the chamber with room to spare.

"Whoahhh!" Alicia said as she fully stepped inside. "What *is* this place?"

"A resting place," Vulcan replied. "For a very old creature. Perhaps the oldest creature of all. Even now, he sleeps. Can you not hear his snoring?"

The sound of rock grinding on rock had grown louder in this chamber, and Alicia looked around. "Where is he?" she asked.

"He is all around us," the Ancient said, gesturing in all directions. "He is the walls, the ceiling. He encases us in his sleeping arms. But I believe it is better that I show you. After countless years, it is time for the sleeping to end. Follow me."

Vulcan walked across the large space, beckoning Alicia to follow, which she did. Eventually, they reached the far wall, a craggy, cracked surface.

"Place your hands on the stone in front of you," Vulcan commanded.

The Rumbling Slumberer

Alicia stepped forward and reached out, resting her palms against the rocky wall. It vibrated with each grinding noise, rattling her bones.

"Now focus," Vulcan said. "Remember the feeling you had when you created the storm? Yes, my sprites saw that, and so I did too. Grab that feeling. Hold it."

Alicia didn't want to "grab that feeling." Not at all. She had been furious. It didn't feel good. "I feel very weak," she said.

"You can do this, Alicia," Vulcan encouraged her. "You are more powerful than you realize. Now go deep inside of yourself and take hold of it."

Alicia sighed and did what the Ancient asked. She remembered her anger at her dad—two dads, actually—and her hatred of Gran'Tree. A tingling began to travel along her arms, and she felt strands of hair lift into the air above her head like it does when you rub a balloon on it.

"Good, good! Now think about the fire. Imagine it forming in your mind. Channel the magic!"

Alicia focused and felt the warmth of the flames spreading from her hand to engulf her. A new sensation was moving through her as the two magics, thunder and fire, combined. It was as if she were caught in a vortex of energy tracing lines on her exposed skin with invisible wires as it spun rapidly around her body. She felt a tingling through her veins as if her blood had turned to carbonated soda.

"Wonderful! Now push that energy. Gently. Push it into the rock before you. Feel it travel through your hands. Push!"

Alicia didn't know exactly what the Ancient meant, but she concentrated and pushed, flattening her palms firmly against the stone. Nothing happened at first. It was almost like the wall was pushing back. Like she was trying to prevent a boulder from rolling downhill and losing the battle. Then something shifted.

The wall before her almost seemed to soften, transform, taking on a jello-like consistency. Her hands felt as if they were sinking into the surface, though visually, nothing of the sort was occurring. She felt the magic start to leave her body, just a trickle at first, then faster, faster, until it was rushing through her fingertips, like the sensation of pulling off a rubber glove, and with a *snap*, it was gone and into the rock wall.

Alicia wobbled on her feet with the release of the magic, wondering if it had worked, and Vulcan moved forward to offer support. Alicia removed her hands from the wall, and together the pair stepped back, waiting, but for what? She did not know.

Suddenly, everything became quiet. The grinding sound, a constant noise since she awakened, ceased. A total and complete silence, similar to being underwater, enveloped them like a blanket. Vulcan guided her daughter back a step further. Alicia's thoughts were frozen with heavy expectation, looking up at the ceiling, around to the sides, and back at the wall in front of her.

Without warning, a deafening sound like thunder broke the silence. A large cloud of dust puffed out from the wall, enveloping Alicia, choking her. The two stumbled back, coughing and covering their ears.

Alicia blinked away the grit filling her eyes and stared back at the stone. A huge crack appeared in the wall before her, running diagonally from near the floor to as high as she could see in the gloomy light. As she watched that crack grew wider, and wider, and wider still.

Alicia stared, not believing what was slowly being revealed. Behind the crack was what appeared to be an eye, the deepest color of green she had ever seen. An eye the size of a house. No, wait, it was continuing to grow. It was getting so large that she was too close to the wall to take in the whole magnitude of it.

Backing away one slow step at a time, she looked up and up as the glistening eye opened wider. After what seemed like an impossibly long time, the noise stopped, and the dust settled. The eye was fully opened.

Removing her hands from her ears, Alicia stood in wonder. As she stared, the massive eye moved, swiveling in its socket. It looked as big as a ten-story building! The enormous pupil in its center, black and empty like the deepest space, narrowed and focused on Alicia. She felt a small rush of fear, and her mouth hung slack.

"HELLO." The voice came, muffled yet tremendously loud, vibrating from deep within the earth causing Alicia to drop to her knees, once again covering her ears.

The rumbling slumberer had awakened.

14

GIGANTIC PROPORTIONS

Alicia, Vulcan, and the sprites made their way quickly back through the darkness of the cave. Alicia brushed the stone dust from her face, still stunned by what she had witnessed. But Vulcan said there was more to come and hustled them along.

Alicia had not realized how deep underground they had been. The air was still, but she could sense motion all around her, a vibration in the air as if the very walls were moving. The sprites lit the way, and she snapped her fingers to summon her own torch in the dark, chasing shadows back like spiders to hide behind rocks and in cubbyholes that shook with small tremors.

Walking and maneuvering through narrow and dimly lit passages took longer than expected before she could finally see the cavern opening ahead, the sunlight blazing through bright and intense. Finally stepping free from the cavern and onto the mountainside, she had to squint her eyes against the glare, waiting for them to adjust.

"Quickly, my child, move!" Vulcan urged her. "We must get down off this mountain. Or I should say, off of Madrigal."

"Mad-what?" Alicia asked, moving as quickly as she could with her temporarily limited vision, following the Ancient—her mother—toward the base of the mountain, not far below where they emerged.

"Not what. Who!" Vulcan was excited again. "Madrigal. One of the few earth giants of the world, maybe even the last. You will see soon enough."

 ## Gigantic Proportions

The ground shook under Alicia, rocking like an earthquake, and it was hard to keep her balance, especially in her already weakened state. She followed Vulcan at breakneck speed, her vision finally clear, glancing over her shoulder and dodging stones that rumbled past her down the hill.

From this vantage point, Alicia had a clear view of the valley below. She could see now that they were in the mountains beyond the east shore of the lake, up above Moose Beach, where she discovered recently her journey started fourteen years ago. When she had been nothing more than an infant. At any other time, she would have stopped to take in the view, but not now.

There were not many trees growing on this slope. It was mostly low brush and grass, so she could move swiftly downhill, despite the constant shaking. Just below, the mountain leveled out into a wide, grassy marshland that extended a hundred yards or more all the way to the edge of the lake. It was there that the Ancient was leading them.

"Hurry, child, hurry!" Sunlight shone off the white, polished surface of Vulcan's skin, reflecting like glittering jewels as she plummeted down, approaching the marsh. Her mother reached the soggy ground and skidded to a halt in the mud, steam rising from her feet.

With long legs moving too fast, Alicia hit the flat ground hard and lost her footing. She tumbled forward past her mother in a very ungraceful somersault, reeling and splashing into the wetlands, a multitude of stones rolling along with her, plunking into the surrounding marsh with watery plops. She came up spluttering and soaking wet.

Vulcan chuckled, watching Alicia, relieved that the water had cushioned the fall. The only thing that appeared to be hurt was her daughter's dignity.

Alicia stood, scowling at the Ancient, and snapped her fingers, bathing herself in fire. She turned up the heat just a touch, drying her hair and clothes quickly.

"Now, *watch!*" Vulcan said, pointing back the way they had come. Alicia waded from the swamp, and turned her eyes expectantly toward the mountainside, waiting, uncertain of what would happen. She did not have to wait long.

With a tremendous eruption of sound that felt like the world was ripping itself apart, the entire range of low foothills spread out before her, tore from the earth. They rose, defying gravity, and lifted slowly into the air a thousand feet or more! Dirt and trees, stones and plants plummeted from base, crashing into the ground below in a cacophony of explosions, kicking up massive plumes of dust. Alicia threw an arm over her head and blinked her eyes rapidly to clear them. The flames coating her fizzled out as she stared, mesmerized by what she was seeing.

The range of hills, now floating in mid-air, was still attached to the rest of the mountain at the farthest end, though she could see to her left that it bent in the middle. The land actually began *bending,* folding in on itself! The hovering end, which was far to her right, moved through the sky coming nearer to where she and the Ancient stood like some giant, elongated airship, then lowered back down toward solid ground. As it did so, Alicia could see the tip begin to split, parts of the land separating, spreading out. What appeared to be an enormous *hand* formed, with thick, rocky fingers and a thumb, at the end of what began to resemble a long, long arm.

The hill—hand—flattened itself on the ground in front of her with an earth-rumbling *boom*, pushed, and suddenly the entire tall mountain range beyond the hills lifted, splitting from the earth, a great thunderous roar pummeling her senses. Alicia could not tear her eyes away from the spectacle as the mountain rose higher and higher into the air, almost touching the clouds!

The shapes Alicia had known her entire life as hills suddenly took on new appearances, reforming themselves in her mind, resolving themselves into other recognizable things. The bending of the land turned into an elbow. A shoulder appeared higher up. And on the mountain top that was reaching for the sky, an enormous head!

With great effort, the earth giant, Madrigal, pushed himself free from the land where he had slept for eons.

"Woooooow . . ." was all Alicia could say. It was unthinkable to imagine a creature so big. Her mind simply could not comprehend. Yet here it was before her, sitting up and blinking those impossibly huge, green eyes.

The giant was stone. He was earthen. He was unbelievable.

"He *is* magnificent," Vulcan said beside her.

The giant surveyed the world before him, blinking his enormous, sleep-filled eyes before turning his colossal head toward the pair, studying them. After several long seconds, he spoke.

"I KNOW YOU," he said, addressing the Ancient, his voice, the grumble of thunder amplified a thousand times.

"Yes, Madrigal, you do. I am Vulcan." She did not raise her voice, but the earth giant seemed to hear her clearly, and Alicia knew there was strong magic at play here. "Though I was much younger last we met, thousands of years ago."

"HAVE I BEEN ASLEEP ALL THIS TIME?" Madrigal asked, blinking his eyes as if seeing for the first time. Alicia noticed his slow, gentle way of speaking that was pleasant to listen to, rich in deep, subtle harmonies, despite the volume. "THE LAKE . . . WAS SO BEAUTIFUL. I SAT TO REST A WHILE AND WATCH."

"You have. So much time has passed and much has changed. But first," the Ancient stepped toward Alicia and put her arm around the girl's shoulders, "I would very much like to introduce you to my daughter, Alicia."

Alicia's mouth was dry from still hanging open, and from the dust the giant's awakening had kicked up. She closed her mouth and swirled her tongue around, tasting dirt before replying, "HELLO, MADRIGAL!"

"You do not have to shout, my child. He can hear you. He is *magic!*"

"HELLO, ALICIA. I SAW YOU IN THE DARK, I THINK. YOU HAVE A GREAT POWER WITHIN YOU. TWO POWERS I CAN SENSE, IT SEEMS. YOU WERE THE ONE TO AWAKEN ME?"

"YES, uh, yes," she replied. "You are . . . breathtaking." The word came out almost as a whisper. "I'm . . . I'm stunned. I'm sorry. I, I don't know what to say." She looked to her mother for help.

"It is alright, child." The Ancient turned back to the earth giant. "My daughter is just discovering her magic," she explained. "Learning to walk, so to speak. Many, many years ago, we Ancients were forced to divide the realms of humankind and magic. The humans had grown . . . greedy over the years, and we were in danger of losing all magic in our lands. And so, a barrier was created. But in the process, we accidentally created an even greater threat than the humans!"

Vulcan looked down at Alicia. "This beautiful young girl was our solution," she went on. "She is my daughter, as well as Thunderbolt's. And as you sensed, she has our powers combined. We believe that she can defeat what threatens to destroy the world. But not alone, not anymore. The threat has grown too strong for any one person to fight."

"AND WHAT IS THIS DANGER?" Madrigal asked. The harmonies in his voice gave the impression that multiple people were talking at just slightly different tones.

Alicia, finding her words again, replied. "It's Gran'Tree. An enormous yellow pine. I weakened him once, many years ago. But now he's feeding on the blood of innocent animals, destroying hundreds of lives. And he's trying to kill me as well." The pleading in Alicia's voice grew as she recounted her story. "Can you help? With you by my side, we can finish him for good. We can't lose!" she said hopefully.

"Do not get too confident yet, child," the Ancient said. "Gran'Tree has grown bigger than you think. The blood he has been drinking . . . it has allowed him to reach gigantic proportions. I have had my sprites spying, and his entire valley is filled with his tremendous roots, stretching across the land like great cables anchoring him to the ground."

Alicia looked up at the massive earth giant. She had thought that Bristleback the mountain troll was big. After all, he had carried her and her companions in his hand. But this creature could easily do the same to Bristleback.

"IF WHAT YOU SAY IS TRUE, I WILL HELP YOU RID THE LAND OF THIS GRAN'TREE," Madrigal said. "ALL CREATURES MUST BE PROTECTED. BUT I NEED SOME TIME TO FULLY

AWAKEN. AFTER THOUSANDS OF YEARS OF SLEEP, MY STRENGTH IS NOT WHAT IT WAS."

The giant paused for a moment. "I WILL ALSO NEED TO ASSEMBLE SOME HELPERS. MY PREVIOUS ONES ARE LONG GONE BY NOW. A CREW, JAY BIRDS, PREFERABLY, BUT ALSO RAVENS. THEY TRAVEL BEFORE ME. AN EARLY WARNING WITH THEIR RAUCOUS CALLS TO ALL THE CREATURES. AN ADVANCE WARNING FOR THEM TO CLEAR A PATH. THIS WAY, I DO NOT STEP ON SOMEONE."

"What a smart idea!" Alicia exclaimed. "I can rest too, and then we can go together. If you'll carry me, that is."

"HA HA HA," the laughter boomed. "NO. A RIDE IN MY HAND WOULD NOT BE PLEASANT FOR ONE SO SMALL AS YOU. MY HANDS ARE NOT SOFT, AND THE RAPID MOVEMENT AND CONSTANT SHAKING COULD HURT YOU."

"And that is why I have another surprise for you, my child," Vulcan said. "Come."

Reluctantly, Alicia tore her eyes from the immense being and followed Vulcan. A tall thicket of brush, overflowing with fluffy fronds, stood nearby, and the Ancient raised her glimmering hand to gesture in its direction. Alicia looked and stopped, frozen in place, watching the creature that emerged from behind the bushes.

"Oh . . . my . . . God! No way! Is that a . . ." She had no more words and approached the creature slowly, extending an arm ever so gently, the existence of the earth giant temporarily forgotten.

The Ancient smiled, watching her daughter's reaction.

Alicia stopped two feet from the creature and reached up hesitantly. "I, I've never seen one! After all these years. Can I . . . I mean . . ."

 ## Gigantic Proportions

An image came into her head then, surprising her. A meadow filled with the most beautiful wildflowers. She remembered a similar image the first time she had met the deer, Fiona, almost exactly the same. She concluded all equines and similar creatures must communicate in this way, through both still and moving pictures "projected" telepathically. A rich bass voice resonated in her head, accompanying the image. "*Yes, you may,*" it said.

Alicia reached higher, stroking the creature's head, and then stretching up on tippy toes; *he was so tall!* Her fingers lightly traced up from the forehead and along the strong curves of the massive antlers, velvety to the touch.

A *moose!*

Alicia laughed. "Ha, ha, *huk!*" almost like a bark, leaped from her throat uncontrollably. She didn't dare to believe it was real, but it was! A moose! Standing right here in front of her! She stepped to the side of the sturdy creature, bigger than any horse, deep brown, with matching brown eyes and long lashes, and stroked her hand along its flank. It was *so strong!* Alicia could feel the large, taut muscles beneath the skin.

A moose! A real live moose! The words kept running through her mind. Despite the name of the nearby beach, she had never actually seen one in real life, and now the laughter continued, high-pitched and giddy and filled with joy. This was a day filled with wonders! She had heard stories, of course. But that is all they had been, just stories. For her, this creature was practically mythical.

The moose was tall, his back maybe six feet high. He had a thick neck and large ears, and his nose and mouth were longer than a horse's. His sturdy legs came up as high as Alicia's chest, and when

she inhaled, she could smell his musky animal scent.

Vulcan smiled, watching Alicia and the large beast. It had taken a bit of searching, there weren't many moose in the area anymore, but she wanted to give this gift to Alicia. A small token of apology for not telling her the truth earlier.

The moose knelt, yet even in this state, he still towered beside Alicia. "*My name is Elenos,*" the voice came into Alicia's head, along with the image of a bed of inviting grasses, clearly a message that she was welcomed aboard.

Alicia ran her hand over the wide back in front of her, feeling the coarse hair on top but a surprisingly soft undercoat below. She reached up with both hands, grabbing hold of the hair that covered the beast's hump to steady herself, being careful not to pull too hard, and then jumped as high as she could, throwing one leg up and over the moose's back.

"Elenos," she said with wonder. "It's a beautiful name. I love it. Thank you."

A warm beam of sunlight filled her head, a sign of pleasure from the moose.

"*You will not need the tools humans use to ride horses with me,*" the moose told her, standing and drawing a "*whoa*" from Alicia as she rocked back slightly and then forward again. "*I will walk gently. Just hold tight to my fur, and you will not slip.*"

Alicia leaned forward and stroked Elenos' soft, thick neck, still finding it incredible that she was *riding a moose!* "Alright, Mads," she called to the giant, remembering once again that he was there but not even looking in his direction. She was still wholly fascinated with this beautiful beast and eager to ride. "We'll go on ahead."

The earth giant looked down at her from where he sat, not fully sure if he was accepting of this new nickname, "Mads," but staying silent for now.

Alicia was energized and excited. Her fever had broken, and the last lingering effects were fading. She was beginning to feel stronger and sensed the magic inside simmering, waiting to be used. She had never been able to summon the storm before, never tried to, really, and now to have felt both magics combined was an incredible rush. She had a sense of renewed hope that, together with her amazing companions, they would annihilate Gran'Tree.

"Let's go," she said to Elenos. "Do you know the way?"

"*Everyone knows the way to Gran'Tree,*" he responded with a note of melancholy, mentally projecting an image of a large valley with a monster rising from the middle. It was terrifying.

Elenos turned, heading south and into the woods that bordered the lake. Alicia looked back before the trees closed around them and waved to Vulcan. "Thank you, thank you, a thousand times thank you!" she called back. She gave a quick wave to Madrigal as well before facing forward again.

"You are so welcome," Vulcan said quietly. "My daughter."

15

ALL IS (TEMPORARILY) RIGHT

Alicia could not stop grinning. Not that she wanted to. This was the happiest she had been in days, maybe even years, and her face hurt from the broad smile that had found a home there.

She wasn't thinking about the danger of Gran'Tree's roots. She wasn't thinking about the lies and deception she had recently discovered. And for that moment, Alicia wasn't thinking about the loss of Tawny either. All she could do was ride her new friend and marvel at how high she was off the ground. It was almost dizzying looking down, but what a view!

The two moved through the coolness of shade trees, the moose stepping over or through bushes with ease. He tried his best to avoid low-hanging branches, but more than a few times, Alicia had to duck or push one aside as they passed. Most importantly, his soft undercoat made the ride quite comfortable.

While she rode, Elenos told stories of the Wild Side Alicia had not heard before. Being a strong, tall creature of the woods, Elenos could go places and travel farther than most. These journeys took him to unique and hidden sanctuaries in the forest.

Alicia heard stories of gnome villages far to the east. The gnomes, she learned, ate nothing but mushrooms. Sometimes they baked them. Sometimes they grilled them. But their favorite was mushroom soup. Gnomes would set a pot over a small campfire early in the morning, adding water and mushrooms along with sage and other local herbs they gathered. The pot simmered low all day,

 ## All is (Temporarily) Right

sending delicious scents drifting out over their small village. As the day progressed, the broth became strong and flavorful just in time for dinner. By far, the best mushrooms were morels which were difficult to find but grew in abundance after a forest fire and were a rare delicacy.

Alicia heard about ogres, which were *very* scary. Ogres were big and lumpy with long hair that was matted with twigs and the dried blood of their victims. They never bathed and smelled horrid, so you always knew when they were nearby. And unlike the troll Bristleback, who only *threatened* to eat people and forest creatures, but who was very gentle, ogres really *did* eat all the animals of the forest. Including humans before the barrier!

Elenos sent images to Alicia's mind of these dark, hulking creatures. She was so very thankful that Elenos could not send smells as well. The pictures were bad enough!

Hours passed, and they eventually stopped to camp for the evening. Alicia was now fearful that an ogre might come hunting them in the night. Still, the moose reassured her, explaining that when The Drying happened, and most of the animals died or moved on, the ogres moved on too, looking for new sources of food. And when The Drying was over, they never desired to move back. Not yet anyway.

At night, Alicia told stories of her own. Tales of exploring as a child and of all the secret spots in the forest that she would visit every year. There was a hidden, icy cold spring, burbling fresh water out of the ground that she was sure only she knew about. It fascinated her to watch the water bubble up and trickle away in a small stream. And there was a large boulder nestled away in the woods spotted with patches of lichen that she would always climb to sit at the top and watch the squirrels play.

Science was a favorite subject of hers, and she excelled at it. Alicia talked about catching tadpoles and keeping them in a small bucket filled with water and stones. She would feed them, watch them lose their tails, and grow legs as they turned into frogs over the course of a couple of weeks, which never ceased to be amazing. She would then release the frogs back into the wild. Elenos, of course, knew about amphibians but kept quiet, letting Alicia speak about them in her own way.

She also talked of her friends back home in the city. Though there were other kids who came to the lake with their families on weekends, Alicia always missed her friends from home during the summer. The previous year, her best friend, Samantha, came to stay at the cabin with Alicia and her family for two weeks. Alicia took her on all the best hikes and was so excited to show Sam some of her favorite magical places.

While Sam had a fun time, and swimming was always a great relief from the July heat, she never seemed to get that sparkle of joy in her eyes that Alicia had in hers. So, her friend did not come back this summer.

Alicia was very much looking forward to starting high school and thought maybe she might meet someone new who shared the same love of the wilderness that she did.

Alicia absolutely loved her journey with Elenos. The moose was amazing, and Alicia got the feeling that he was quite old, though he appeared strong and energetic. His stories left the impression that he had seen many of these things himself and was not just repeating

tales handed down through generations. And though Alicia never asked directly, it could be considered impolite to ask an older person (or moose in this case) their age, Alicia did discover that Elenos had lived an extraordinarily long and beautiful life.

Alicia didn't want this ride to end, but after a couple of days at their gentle yet steady pace, she knew they were getting close to the valley of Gran'Tree. In fact, she had begun to see more and more of the piles of woven sticks, hundreds of them. She knew the gruesome contents they held and was horrified by what that meant. The great yellow pine's power was growing. She tried to avoid looking at them and thinking about the problem the stick piles created, but they were so numerous now it was impossible to ignore the truth. Her anger began to return, still buried inside, but she was aware of it now.

Sure enough, on the morning of the third day, a massive flock of jays came zipping through the forest branches. Alicia recognized the familiar speech pattern from her time spent with Briar. "*CAW!* Get out of the *CAW* way! Move, move, move! An earth *CAW* giant is coming! *CAW*"

Alicia and Elenos felt Madrigal's coming from the vibrations in the ground long before they saw him. Moving out of the woods and into a large clearing where their view was no longer obstructed by the branches of the trees, they could see his approach as his head and shoulders towered above the forest. Alicia slid off the moose and brought forth her fire magic, waving her arms and sending flames crackling high above her head so that Madrigal could see them easily.

The giant slowed his approach and stopped, looking down at the two of them. "HELLO AGAIN," he said. "I FEEL RESTED."

This was the first time Alicia had seen the earth giant standing at his full height. She thought he was big when she first saw him, but now, her eyes could barely take in his whole size. He was sort of gorilla-shaped, a dusty tan and grey in color, with long arms that hung down far below his waist. His skin was rocky, and his stumpy legs were much shorter than expected. And those dazzling green eyes were impressive. This creature was old beyond reckoning, and she agreed with Vulcan. He *was* magnificent!

Alicia let the fire surrounding her dim and called to him, "I'M RESTED TOO! OH, SORRY. Sorry." She stopped yelling. "I forgot that you can hear me just fine."

"I CAN," the giant replied.

"The ride here has been perfect," Alicia said. Glancing at the moose she smiled warmly. "Elenos has been great company."

Elenos lowered his head and nuzzled her neck, sending an image of rosy flower blooms. *Is that his way of blushing?* Alicia thought, surprised that a beast so strong could be moved by her words. *Cuuuute!*

Madrigal raised a long arm and pointed in the direction they were traveling. "I BELIEVE I CAN SEE THE YELLOW PINE YOU WERE TALKING ABOUT FROM HERE. HE IS *VERY* BIG. HIS CROWN IS HIGHER THAN THE RIM OF THE VALLEY. HE APPEARS TO BE EVEN TALLER THAN ME."

Oh my, Alicia thought. *If Gran'Tree is that big, he must have grown at an unbelievable rate!* Alicia remembered all the stick piles she had seen along the way, which gave her a sense of just how much blood the tree had absorbed. If there was magic in the blood, as The Silver King had thought, Gran'Tree must be incredibly powerful. She felt her fury come on strong again at the thought of all that death, and her fire flared up. Alicia knew that the fight ahead would not be easy.

"There is a pass that leads through the mountain to the valley right there." Alicia pointed ahead, indicating the small crevasse in the line of mountains before them. "Elenos and I will ride there and stop before going down into the valley. We can take a look and talk about the best plan from there. Ok?"

"OH KAY?" Madrigal looked confused.

Alicia suddenly wondered if that was a real word or just something made up. "Ok," she repeated. "It means, uh, something like, is that a good idea? Do you think that plan works? You are supposed to respond with 'ok' if you agree with me."

"I THINK I UNDERSTAND NOW. OH KAY. THAT PLAN WORKS."

"Alright, Mads. We will see you there!" Elenos knelt again, letting Alicia clamber back up, and together they headed toward the mountains and the narrow pass there.

"YES, ALL IS RIGHT. I WILL SEE YOU THERE TOO." With his long arms, Madrigal carefully lowered himself to the ground to wait, his stubby legs sticking out in front of him, allowing the Ancient's daughter and her companion to go first, not wanting to accidentally injure them with his walking. "ALL IS RIGHT. I HOPE."

16

A SOFTLY SIMMERING ANGER

Alicia sat on Elenos' back, looking out over the valley ahead of her. Madrigal was right. Gran'Tree was *very* big. In fact, even saying "very big" was kind of an understatement.

The entire valley below was overtaken by Gran'Tree's roots. They writhed and pulsed like tentacles as if the tree had become a hybrid of plant and animal. It looked like the valley was filled with giant eels. In some places, the roots grew so fat that they split, oozing a reddish fluid –blood?– thick like glue, down their wooden sides. The vile, tacky liquid soaked into the ground, staining the visible sections of the valley floor a patchy crimson color. A coppery sour stench of blood and death hung heavy in the air.

And rising from the center of it all, like a living skyscraper of wood, was Gran'Tree himself, the mighty yellow pine, now become a towering behemoth. A destroyer of worlds.

This was not the tree she faced just a few short weeks ago. That tree was shrunken and withered, weakened to the point of death. This wasn't even the tree she had met three years ago, which had been extremely large and majestic, but nothing more than uncaring and indifferent to those creatures around him, as if the only thing that mattered at all was himself.

No, this tree was monstrous! Pure evil. His crown of branches rose above the line of the mountain range, as Madrigal had said, brushing the clouds. His face was hideous. While always frightening, with a huge gash for a mouth and two large knots for eyes, now it was malevolent and had grown along with the rest of the tree.

A Softly Simmering Anger

The jagged maw was big enough to swallow a bus, and where sap, leaking from the edges of his mouth, had previously formed yellow streaks down the trunk, now those streaks had a hint of crimson in them. The outside corners of both knotty eyes flared upwards as if looking over the destruction he had wrought gave the yellow pine great pleasure.

"What have I done?" Alicia spoke the question aloud, but it was only directed at herself. Her shoulders sagged as she looked across the dead valley, and she repeated the question slowly. "What have I done?"

She saw an image in her head of a moose calf being cared for by its mother. The concern was obvious. *Was this Elenos as a child, she wondered?* More likely simply the way the moose showed that he cared for the girl.

"*This is not your fault, Alicia,*" Elenos said. "*You cannot take the blame for the actions of others.*"

"But I *told* him about my blood. About The Silver King trying to take it. I told him there was *magic* in the blood! I was terribly right . . ." Her voice faded.

"*Each of us is responsible for our choices, good or bad,*" Elenos insisted. "*If you tell a friend how much joy you get from the colors of a flower, and then they get joy from another flower, are you responsible for that happiness?*"

"No," Alicia said.

"*You also spoke of your friend who visited but who did not feel the same as you about the magical places. You tried to show her, but she did not share your excitement. Do you feel responsible for that?*"

"No, but . . ." Alicia started to say.

"*No, you do not, and you should not,*" Elenos responded gently.

"*We are all unique beings responsible for our actions,*" Elenos continued. "*Never place blame on others for your own actions. Likewise, you should not blame yourself for the actions of another.*"

"But *I* broke the barrier! *I* did that! *I* gave him access to the human realm. And now he could destroy the world!"

Fear of what she had unleashed on this earth tickled the back of her neck and raised the hair along her arms. Along with that, the softly simmering anger Alicia had felt since first seeing the vast number of stick piles and learning of all the drained and withered animals within them began to grow in intensity.

Fire blossomed in her hand, and she quickly scrambled off of Elenos' back. She knew that the fire would only do what she wanted, but she also remembered the scorched ground beneath her feet. She still did not feel fully in control of the magic and she feared unintentionally harming the moose.

Elenos turned his long face to look at her. "*Yes, you broke the barrier between worlds,*" he agreed. "*You did what you had to do to save your parents. But the actions of Gran'Tree since then, what he has done to the creatures of the Wild Side? You cannot and should not take responsibility for that.*"

The fire bloomed brighter in her hand and continued to spread across Alicia's body as her rage continued to grow. The light coming from above began to dim as dark clouds started forming over the tops of the mountain range surrounding this valley of horrors.

A voice filled with malice rolled, rumbling across the land. "Iii see youuu, Aliiiciaaa. Youuu caaame." The light from her magic must have given her away, standing out like a spotlight in the growing darkness. Gran'Tree knew she had arrived, and there was no more hiding.

A Softly Simmering Anger

The voice was loud and croaky like an unpleasant toad. Perhaps not quite as loud as Madrigal's, but still blaring across the valley like a siren. Yet at the same time, the words were spoken almost in a whisper. The way they were drawn out hummed in the air around her, lingering like plucked guitar strings.

"Iii haaave taaasted youuur bloood," Gran'Tree said, mocking her. "Aaand, Iii haaave taaasted theee bloood of youuur faaather tooo. Aaand youuur *cat!*" Gran'Tree barked out the last word. "Viiicious thiiing! Suuuch a shaaame sheee is not heeere wiiith youuu."

The sharp words cut her heart as easily as a knife, and a low rumble of thunder echoed through the mountains as Alicia's anger grew.

"I AM HERE, ALICIA." The new voice caught her off guard. She had been so focused on listening to Gran'Tree, that she hadn't even noticed the earth giant climbing up, filling the canyon pass behind her with his massive bulk. She looked back and high up into his green eyes.

"All is *not* right," she said through clenched teeth.

"NO," Madrigal agreed. "ALL IS NOT RIGHT."

"Oooh, youuu brouuught frieeends," Gran'Tree said. "Dooo youuu meeean tooo caaause meee haaarm? Dooo not foool youuurself, *chiiiild!*"

Alicia heard the disdain in his voice as he spoke the final word, reverberating in the air around them. As if she was an insignificant bug. Nothing to be bothered with. *He could not be more wrong,* she thought.

"Iii aaam *not* theee ooone youuu met yeeears agooo," Gran'Tree said. "Theeen, Iii caaared *nooothing* fooor the creeeatuuures of thiiis wooorld. Theyyy weeere smaaall, meeeaniiingleeess. Nooow! Thooose creeeatuuures giiive meee myyy streeength. Myyy pooower! Youuu wiiill NOT taaake *that* frooom meee agaaain!"

Gran'Tree's roots became agitated, causing the valley floor to appear alive with gigantic, blood-filled worms, thrashing and roiling against one another. The great tree gave the tiniest of shakes, and suddenly the air was filled with millions of pine needles, whistling as they flew like tiny daggers toward her and her companions.

Alicia gave a push to her fire magic, and she was immediately enveloped by the flames. The pine needles burned away in a multitude of sparks as they crashed against her. They bounced harmlessly off the giant as well. Elenos was not so lucky.

Alicia heard a bellow of pain and looked quickly at the moose. Elenos was covered with small lacerations, and hundreds of pine needles were stuck in the hair along the side of his body, which faced the tree.

Thunder *cracked* through the valley, and rain began to fall. Fat droplets hit the fire that wreathed Alicia and sizzled with little "tsss" sounds as they evaporated. She reached forward, placing her hands on the moose, allowing her fire to cover Elenos. The needles embedded in his flank burned and fell away, leaving behind numerous small bloody dots that healed rapidly.

"*Do not worry, Alicia,*" Elenos sent. "*I have a natural healing ability, and the wounds will not last. But I cannot take repeated attacks like that. I am sorry, I will not be able to continue into the valley with you.*"

"I can protect you," Alicia said. "I can keep you covered in flames that will stop the needles."

"*No, you must understand your limits,*" he sent, creating an image in her mind of a young bird learning to fly. "*Under normal circumstances, I might agree. But these are far from normal.*" Elenos looked at

Gran'Tree. *"He is more powerful than even I knew. You have the magic of the Ancients in you. He has the blood of a thousand animals in him, and there is magic in that. You know it. You will need to focus more than ever without worrying about me. Go do what you must."*

Elenos then looked up at Madrigal. Alicia couldn't hear what he said to the giant; the message was sent only to him, but she could hear the giant's rumbling response. "I WILL."

Alicia looked back down into the valley, her eyes landing on the huge piles of sand not far away, strewn among the undulating roots of the great tree. All that remained of her friend, Bristleback. She spoke up loudly then, addressing Gran'Tree for the first time.

"Gran'Tree, I am not the one you met years ago, either! You will pay for all the death you have caused!" Her voice quietly echoed from the thunder that rolled through the valley, "*caused . . . caused . . . caused,*" as if there were speakers embedded in the clouds, a softly growling repetition of her words. The fire burned brightly around her, and a bolt of lightning crashed into the ground halfway between Alicia and the yellow pine, just barely missing one of the great roots.

"You've killed so many animals, taken so many lives. You've gained your power, stolen it, through the destruction of those too weak to fight. I don't believe your greed for power will *ever* end. *End . . . end . . . end . . .*"

She glanced back quickly at the piles of sand below and once again at Gran'Tree.

"And you are responsible for the death of two of my dear friends. I can never forgive that, and I hate you for it. *I hate you!*" she screamed.

Hate you, hate you, hate you, the echo came back as more thunder filled the sky, and the rain increased in intensity. It had no effect on Alicia's cloak of fire, which blazed like a raging furnace, stoked by her anger. She had learned to control both powers simultaneously.

"Theeen cooome, *child*. Weee wiiill fiiiniiish this!"

Alicia looked up at Madrigal. "Let's do this," she said.

"LET US DO THIS!"

17

A CLASH OF TITANS

Alicia moved down the mountain pass, a small cascade of pebbles rolling along the path beside her, and reached the stained valley floor. At the same time, Elenos stepped off to the side, where he could be protected from additional needle attacks. Madrigal waited until she and the moose were clear before stepping carefully through the pass to join Alicia.

Except for the yellow pine, nothing lived here. Nothing *could* live here. The grass and wildflowers that had once filled the valley with a beautiful meadow were decimated and the creatures had either fled or been consumed.

Ahead of her lay the giant roots of the tree, flexing and dripping vile fluids, blocking her path to the tree. They were far too big for her to clamber over, and threading her way between them would be like trying to navigate a labyrinth.

"Whaaat iiis the maaatter, liiittle giiirl? Caaannot reeeach meee?" Gran'Tree taunted. "Whaaat a shaaame. Buuut, Iii caaan reeeach youuu!" With that, several stick vines she now understood were roots burst forth from the ground around Alicia and tried to wrap themselves around her. They burned to ash as soon as they struck her armor of fire.

"HAH!" Alicia screamed at Gran'Tree with hateful glee. She let the anger fill her and stretched a hand to the sky, calling down a bolt of lightning directly above the great tree. The bolt struck the crown of the tree, snapping branches and sending bits of bark and needles flying in all directions, but it couldn't break through the tree's thick barrier.

Alicia called down two more bolts in rapid succession, but neither could smash through the heavy, mutated limbs, though she did see a curl of smoke rising from one. Breathing heavily from the exertion of supporting two types of magic, she felt some small satisfaction. She had hurt him like he had hurt Elenos. *Payback!*

"Aaarrrrgh!" the great yellow pine screamed and shook harder, sending pine needles flying their way. And once again, they burned to ashes as they hit Alicia and bounced off of Madrigal's stony skin.

"Is that all you can do?" Alicia taunted in return, infused with a sense of satisfaction.

"Iiit loooks liiike weee aaare at an immmpaaasse," Gran'Tree said. "Buuut youuu wiiill tiiire ouuut looong befooore Iii wiiill. Hooow much enerrrgyyy doooes it taaake to keeep that maaagic goiiing? Hooow much enerrrgyyy caaan ooone *chiiild* hold? Iii haaave the enerrrgyyy frooom the bloood of thouuusands flooowing throuuugh meee, and mooore accesssssible at anyyy tiiime frommm myyy rooots spreeead acrooosss thiiis laaand."

The tree paused, letting the words sink in, then continued its evil threats. "Mayyybe Iii wiiill driiink frommm youuur motherrr neeext. Theeere in youuur liiittle cabiiin, waaaiting for youuu to cooome hooome. Iii caaan feeel her theeere. Paaaciing theee flooorbooooards. Mayyybe Iii wiiill driiink her DRYYY!"

"NO!" Alicia screamed, fury taking hold of her. Gathering all her strength, she summoned another tremendous, jagged bolt of lightning. It flashed down and struck the top of Gran'Tree like a giant wedge, driving through the crown of branches and hitting the thick trunk of the tree with incredible force. A great *BOOM* of thunder shook the valley, accompanied by an ear-splitting *CRACK*,

as Gran'Tree's massive trunk split right down the middle from the top to just above that horrific face.

Gran'Tree screamed in pain and his huge roots thrashed violently, forcing Alicia to dodge quickly out of their way. Great streams of reddish-brown sap flowed from the split in his head, like lava pouring from the top of a volcano. Dark smoke curled into the sky, and bright red embers glowed atop Gran'Tree for a moment but were quickly dying out from the downpour of rain.

Bent over, hands on knees, trying to recover her strength, Alicia yelled, "NOW, MADS! TAKE HIM OUT!"

The earth giant, who had been watching the exchange waiting for the right time, stepped forward through the wide valley, trampling across roots. It only took him a couple of strides and he reached the tree, wrapping his extra-long arms around the thick trunk. Madrigal pulled, but he couldn't budge Gran'Tree. The tentacle-like roots anchored the great tree solidly to the valley floor and beyond.

"UUUUUHHHH!" The giant heaved, but nothing was happening. Shifting position, he tried rocking the trunk back and forth, side to side, but just could not dislodge the tree.

Suddenly, one of the enormous roots ripped free from the ground. "Yes!" Alicia exclaimed, watching as Madrigal successfully tore loose an anchor. But she was mistaken in that assumption.

The bloody, dripping root rose high into the air and then slithered around the giant's waist. It pulled, but Madrigal's arms were firmly wrapped around the tree. Another grotesque root dragged itself from the ground, lifted, and curled around the giant like an octopus seizing its prey, followed by two more, encircling the ancient creature's legs. The two titans almost appeared to be hugging one another in a most dangerous embrace.

Alicia saw the roots around the waist of the earth giant go taut as Gran'Tree increased his pull, and she watched Madrigal's hands slipping from the tree. The earth giant adjusted his grip, holding more tightly than ever, granite hands grasping at the wet bark. Two more of the tree's roots dislodged themselves from the valley floor, wrapping firmly around Madrigal's upper arms like chains. With these two more added to what had come before, the giant's grip began to weaken, and Alicia watched helplessly as he began to tip backward. He tried to take a step back to maintain his balance, but his legs were locked in place by the massive roots there. He couldn't move them!

His balance lost, Alicia watched in despair as the great giant tipped, slowly at first but gaining momentum. She threw her hands over her head, ducking behind a nearby root as the living mountain came crashing down beside her. The shockwave of the impact shook the entire valley and hit Alicia like an explosion, sending her tumbling head over heels through the mottled dirt.

Lying unmoving and face down on the ground, she went through a mental checklist. *Ok, I'm dizzy but conscious*, Alicia thought. She slowly flexed her fingers, then her arms and legs. Nothing seemed to be broken, but she had cuts and scrapes everywhere. And bruises she knew she would feel for a very long time.

Alicia pushed herself into a sitting position, looking over her body to see if there was anything bleeding more than it should—or at least, more than she could survive. Nothing too bloody was visible. She also saw the fire, though dim, still surrounding her. That was good.

She turned her eyes toward the carnage before her, but nothing was visible. Dust still hung in the air, obscuring her vision. The rain was a persistent force and quickly washed it down. Alicia struggled slowly and painfully to her feet as the air cleared and scanned the valley, shocked at what she saw.

Madrigal lay on the ground in front of her, his arms, legs, and chest bound by the roots of Gran'Tree. The earth giant, huge beyond belief, had been completely immobilized by the sheer number and mass of the disgusting roots. The most he could do was turn his head, which he did now, looking at her.

"I AM SORRY," he said. "I DID WHAT I COULD. HE IS JUST TOO STRONG. MUCH TOO STRONG."

Alicia stood battered, scraped, bruised, and exhausted. The fire armor surrounding her was dying out, and rain was getting through in spots, wetting her hair and clothes. Her anger and use of the new magics simultaneously drained her. But she had to try. There was no giving up!

Alicia raised her arm once more and watched as the rain washed streaks of red dirt down into her shirt sleeve. She looked to the sky above Gran'Tree and at the dark clouds that resided there. She would have one shot at this, she thought. One shot to get this exactly right. If she could guide a bolt of lightning directly into the crack that she had created, maybe, *just maybe* she could drive it all the way to the heart of this horrid creature. Maybe she could end his destructive growth. Maybe she could save the realm, *both* realms. Her parents. The world.

Standing in the rain, knowing she no longer had the strength to maintain both magics simultaneously, Alicia reluctantly let what remained of her fire shield drop and extinguish. Immediately, Gran'Tree's small roots burst up through the ground at Alicia's feet and began to shroud her legs with their deadly wrappings.

She remained focused, ignoring the climbing roots and repeated stabs of pain in her legs as the great tree began to feed on her blood. Alicia channeled the energy she had been drawing on to keep the fire shield and sent it traveling through her raised arm instead. She felt as if she were holding a small hummingbird, its wings vibrating a hundred beats a second as the magic gathered in her hand. The storm cloud above Gran'Tree grew darker still as the roots reached her waist and climbed higher.

Alicia screamed, tearing her throat raw with the force of it, hearing the echo from the thunderclouds filling the valley. With all her rage, Alicia called down the electricity from the cloud that hung above the tree and focused it—every single volt—sending it with laser precision, seeking a path directly down the center, threading a needle between the branches, through the crack, and into the terrible heart of Gran'Tree.

Except, that's not what happened. Not at all.

Gran'Tree had been watching the girl, feeling the intense pain of the burning in his trunk from her previous strike. He saw what she was doing and knew with certainty what she intended. He waited, feeling the energy coalesce in the cloud above him, the static charge of electricity building and tingling his limbs. Sensing the lightning strike to come, Gran'Tree threw up his highest branches, sheathing his trunk and the dripping wound there, protecting it from her magic.

When the strike came, it was powerful. But the great tree was more powerful still, and this time Gran'Tree was prepared. His branches absorbed the energy of the lightning bolt, some catching fire and exploding into fragments. But the majority remained, protecting the great tree's heart. The lightning traveled down the side of the tree and into the earth, stripping great chunks of bark from its trunk along the way. But only enough to damage, not enough to destroy. The rain came down hard, extinguishing the remaining flames.

Alicia watched this happen, drained of all remaining strength, terror and disbelief shrouding her face. She was a wet towel, wrung of lifeforce. The weight of her failure was heavy as she hung her head. Rain poured down around her, and in that moment, all hope was lost. She was defeated. The roots slowly engulfed her, slithering higher along her back and chest. Alicia tipped forward and fell, her face slamming into the muddy, red ground.

Laughter rumbled across the rain-soaked valley, deep and quiet but growing in volume.

"Iii tooold youuu not to chaaallenge meee!" Gran'Tree was shouting now, filled with the satisfaction of his triumph over the young witch. "Diiid youuu reaaally think youuu couuuld defeeeat meee??!! Iii aaam the mooost pooowerfuuul beiiing that eveeer liiived!! Aaand youuu aaare juuust aaa LIIITTLE GIIIRL! HAAAA HAAAA HAAAA HAAA!!"

The laughter continued as the roots wrapped themselves cruelly around Alicia's arms, her shoulders, her neck. The pricks of pain were everywhere now, the thin white roots burrowing beneath her skin, tapping into her veins, draining her of her blood. Her magic. Her life.

The roots snaked through Alicia's wet hair and along her scalp. They slid across her cheeks. She couldn't move; her limbs were pinned tightly to the muddy ground. As the roots began to block her vision, she closed her eyes in defeat. The last thing Alicia heard before her head was fully encased was the laughter of the evil tree. And then, she heard nothing.

18

LOST LOVE

Word spread at the speed of sound.

The ravens and jays that had accompanied Madrigal to the valley, spreading the message of his coming, just as quickly spread the message of his defeat. And with that came a message of despair. Of warning. The Burning Girl had fallen, and Gran'Tree still lived.

The ravens carried the message to the robins, who carried the message to the deer, who carried the message to the squirrels, who carried the message to the pixies, who carried their fateful message to Vulcan.

All hope was lost. The grand plan, devised thousands of years ago, their one hope to restore the realm, had failed. The tree lived. Her daughter was gone.

Vulcan bowed her head in sorrow and shame for sending Alicia to do what she could not. She sank to her knees and remained there motionless, engulfed in billowing clouds of steam rising from the hot springs she called home. In the surrounding woods, the ground stirred with the wriggling of roots.

The message continued like a tidal wave through the land, splashing against the tall shores of Thunderbolt's mountain. The Ancient stepped from his ramshackle home and walked to the edge of the plateau to stare across the land from his mountain peak.

Lost Love

How long before Gran'Tree's roots find their way to me? If my daughter, a child of the Ancients who could wield such magics, has fallen to the tree, what hope is there?

He turned his eyes skyward, tracking the sun's path. *This is the end of the world*, he thought. *Soon, there will be nothing left to consume. Maybe then, the great enemy we created will no longer exist. And maybe then, the world can be reborn.*

He turned to shuffle back to his home, pausing one last time to look back. "I hope the new world is better," he sighed. "I hope there is love."

Thunderbolt entered the dark cabin, added another log to the wood stove, and waited for the inevitable.

The darkness was crushing, suffocating. The thick, rough roots wrapped and squeezed and pinched her skin, while thinner ones pierced her arms, legs, and back. They pulsed gently, almost in rhythm with her heart, as they slowly siphoned her blood.

Alicia's anger had exhausted her. She was weak from the magic and now her remaining energy was being drained away, along with her blood, to feed the great tree. She felt sleepy, her mind slowly losing consciousness, and the valiant warrior wondered which would kill her first—the lack of oxygen or the loss of blood.

Gran'Tree had won. He was right. She had been foolish to challenge him. He was more powerful than anyone knew or could have believed. But what choice did she have? She was the tool, wasn't she? The weapon conceived for this purpose alone. She had helped to create this mess; she had to try and set it right. To fix what she had done.

Alicia's short life flitted through her foggy mind. She thought that maybe she'd gotten that "fixer" quality from her dad. Not Thunderbolt, but rather the person who had been there to help raise her, take her on hikes, and introduce her to the wonders of the wilderness. And despite *how* Alicia was born, *Richard* was her dad. She regretted intensely that her last conversation with him had been angry, shouted words.

And her mom. Alicia knew that was where she got her smarts and her love for reading. From Kate, not Vulcan. She remembered nights falling asleep, snuggled up against her mother's warm body, listening to the fantastical stories her mother read. *The Jungle Book, A Wrinkle in Time, Charlotte's Web.* They would inevitably fill Alicia's sleeping head with dreams. All of this was lost to her now. Lost forever.

This is where dreams go to die, she thought. She had heard those words somewhere before and felt nothing could be more real for her and her family, which would soon be devoured by the great tree. Now all she could hear was the heartbeat in her ears. A muffled *whump whump . . . whump whump . . .* slowing, slowing. She was so sleepy.

As she continued to slip into cold unconsciousness, feeling the constant sting of the roots embedded in her flesh and latched onto veins, relentlessly drinking, *sip sip sip*, Alicia became aware of another movement. This wasn't from the roots feeding on her. No, this movement came from outside. A sound penetrated through the muffled quiet of her deadly prison. It was a sort of scratching sound. And then . . . a snarl.

Suddenly, there was a grey light. Just a sliver, the tiniest glimmer shining through the wooden cage around Alicia's head, hitting her eye and constricting the pupil, but it was there. Growling came from close by, followed by a slashing sound, like a scythe cutting through a field of wheat, and just like that, her head was free.

Weak and confused, her eyes blurry, Alicia saw a shape darting back and jumping forward again to slash at another part of her body, cutting through more of the roots that were holding her to the ground. Back and forth, back and forth, almost faster than she could see, dodging the roots that burst from the ground around her. And then the creature paused just for a moment to look at her, and Alicia could finally see clearly. Two black scars running along a neck of yellow fur and *two shining golden eyes.*

Tawny!

The cougar leapt forward again, slashing more of the entangling roots away from Alicia's chest. Encouraged, Alicia tried to draw on the magic one more time and felt it there, weak but still in her. Concentrating with all her might, she raised a wet and bloody hand and snapped her fingers. A flame appeared, faint and flickering, like a flashlight with dying batteries.

She dragged her burning hand across the rest of the roots covering her legs. They caught fire and thrashed, pulling away from the flame and retreating into the ground. She could feel the thinner roots that had burrowed beneath her skin withdrawing, like the pulling out of long splinters. Small points of pain remained, bleeding gently and stinging sharply, but she was free!

Turning, she crawled quickly to the massive cat, a welcome and unexpected sight, and threw her arms around the furry neck she so loved. Alicia let the fire cover her and gently guided it over Tawny as well. The cat pulled frantically, eyes wide, struggling as she tried to escape the flames that had no heat. Then, the realization slowly dawning on her that there was no pain, she cautiously settled into the tight embrace, rubbing her cheek fiercely against the girl.

"How?" Alicia sobbed. Great tears of joy flowed down her face. "I saw you fall. I watched you die!"

But as she thought back to that moment, Alicia realized she never found the cat after Tawny fell. Maybe the great cat caught herself on one of the many trees below, snagging onto a tree branch with her sharp claws. Maybe Tawny landed in the river and, somehow, managed to survive long enough to pull herself to shore. Alicia would never know for sure. All she knew was that a miracle must have happened.

Tawny purred loudly, and Alicia hugged tighter.

"I searched, and you weren't there. I ran down the mountain. I ran and fell, but I kept on running to find you." Tears continued to flow down Alicia's cheeks.

"You were gone. You were just . . . gone! Oh, Tawny, I love you. I love you so much! I'm never letting you go again!"

Alicia's heart swelled with emotion, feeling as if it was going to explode. Like her chest couldn't contain this feeling. It was almost a struggle to breathe as if her heart was pushing on her lungs, trying to make room for extra growth.

With Tawny's love, her power came flooding back, along with a sudden and profound understanding.

What had people been telling her this whole time? Love was the missing element. Alicia had been born but incomplete. There was no *love!* It was why she had been delivered to the realm of humankind in the first place. Why her mother, Vulcan, made such a difficult choice to give up her only child.

  ## Lost Love

Until now, all Alicia had been feeling was anger. Anger at being deceived by her parents. *All four* of them. Anger at the loss of Tawny. Anger at Gran'Tree and his murderous ways. She thought she could control that anger, use it somehow. She came to this valley to annihilate the great yellow pine, but for the wrong reasons. Alicia had hated the tree for the deaths he caused; for his need to be powerful, regardless of the damage done along the way. She still did, but hate was not a reason to destroy him. She shouldn't want to fight Gran'Tree because of hate. Not for vengeance. That was the lesson she had needed to learn. She wanted to defeat him because of love. Because she *loved* all the other creatures of the realms.

This sudden understanding swept through her and she embraced it, letting it fill her, energize her, strengthen her body and her magic. Gran'Tree was devouring the creatures of this land, and they needed a defender. They needed the Burning Girl. They needed her!

Tawny was here, beyond all belief, somehow returned to her. Alicia pulled away from the cat, keeping her hands on Tawny's thick shoulders so the fire would continue covering her. Protecting her. Looking into the cat's golden eyes, she said, "I love you, Tawny, like I love my mom and my dad. And I love all the amazing creatures I have met in this world. And I don't want anything bad to happen to any of you. And for *that* reason, I will defeat Gran'Tree."

She wiped her eyes and continued. "Thank you for saving me. And thank you for helping me understand. I can never repay you for that. But I can repay the world for giving you back to me." She looked toward Gran'Tree, who was no longer laughing. Only watching and waiting, his powerful energy surrounding them.

"Bob the bear said hate could destroy me," she said, turning to the cat. "He was right. It almost did. But now I know the truth. Anger drains you. It's exhausting. But love," she stroked the cat, "love does just the opposite. It fills you! It energizes your whole being."

Alicia smiled, feeling renewed. "You reminded me of that just now. So, thank you, Tawny. But I need you to go. Leave. Go somewhere safe. Find some rocks and stay on them. Just get far away." Alicia looked back at Gran'Tree. "I need to finish this."

Alicia stood and turned to face the great yellow pine. She heard Tawny moving and glanced over her shoulder to make sure the cat was leaving, which she was, quickly.

The Burning Girl once again faced Gran'Tree. She summoned the energy vortex and felt the carbonated sensation in her veins again.

And she began to sing.

19

SOMEWHERE, A LEGEND DIES

A quiet had settled across the land. With the passing of the messengers, the ravens, the robins, the squirrels, a hush filled the air like the moments before a storm. It was as if all the creatures of the woods had reached acceptance. They were mourners, leaving a funeral with the heavy knowledge that life was short, and that Gran' Tree would be coming for them all.

Into this silence, a faint sound emerged. Like the string section of an orchestra just starting to warm up before a performance. Except these notes were not random. Rather, they formed a melody, pure and clean as a mountain stream, flowing like water through the valleys and canyons, sweeping between the branches of the pine trees, and seeping down to carve channels through the bushes and wildflowers.

An old bear raised his head from the patch of berries he was enjoying and listened. "Finally," he grumbled to no one in particular. "She finally understands."

The bear lowered his grizzled head back into the bushes, continuing his search for the last remaining berries left over from the bountiful summer. But he couldn't stop a small smile from ticking up the corners of his great mouth.

Somewhere in a southern valley, lightning spiked across the sky.

Somewhere, A Legend Dies

A bushy-tailed red fox held a chubby squirming squirrel on its back. The chase had been intense but quick, and now he was preparing to feast. But before he could eat, the fox paused, listening.

He heard a melody floating through the air, drifting quietly over the treetops and down to blanket the forest floor. He had never heard anything like it.

Looking down at the squirrel, the fox considered, then slowly raised his paw. "You got lucky this time," the fox hissed through pointed teeth. "But if I find you again . . ." The fox snapped his jaws together twice with a sharp *"clack clack"* and licked his black lips. The squirrel, hearing the music as well, righted himself. "Thank you!" he breathed, then ran as fast as his short legs would take him back to his family.

Somewhere in a southern valley, flames sizzled along bare arms.

Two jaybirds were having an argument about which one stole the other's food, a common argument among jays, and neither one was winning. Both stopped their raucous "*CAW*ing" at each other and perked up, heads tilted to the side. A voice, filled with song, floated towards their ears. It was so pleasant and much nicer than their arguing.

The jays settled down together on their branch, food forgotten, listening to the notes that drifted through the air.

Somewhere in a southern valley, deep thunder shook the wet ground.

An Ancient made of mud huddled in the darkness with his repulsive "pets." He listened to the music reverberate off the walls and through his cave. The music was filled with power that he craved and almost had once but let slip through his misshapen fingers.

He knew the source, and it infuriated the Ancient. His lingering magic caused a small tremor to shake his domain, dropping filthy leeches from the ceiling and creating new cracks along the damp walls that surrounded him.

The Ancient sat on his silver throne and fumed in anger.

Somewhere in a southern valley, a cat tucked her head low and ran.

A man and a woman sat terrified in their small cabin, waiting and praying for good news. Music drifted in through an open window, quietly at first but getting louder.

They listened closely and looked at each other, eyes filled with wonder and beginning to spill over with tears. They *knew* that song.

 Somewhere, A Legend Dies

The man and the woman hugged each other tightly and knew in their hearts their daughter was alive.

In a valley, somewhere far to the south, a girl cloaked in flames stood facing a tree of immense size. A Goliath. And she sang beautifully.

If you ever, ever feel like cryin'
'Cause the whole world, seems like they've been lyin'
You can call me, call me and I'll be there
You can call me, and I'll show you just how much I care
I'll let the light in
Yeah, I'll let the light in

Gran'Tree looked on with disdain. "Youuu triiied thaaat trick befooore. Thaaat wooon't affeeect meee thiiis tiiime. Youuu seee, Iii haaave to caaare fooor that to wooork. Aaand, Iii dooo not. Not fooor youuu. Not fooor anyyythiiing!"

But still, Alicia sang on. It was a song her father had written, and one that used to be sung around campfires when she was younger. The memories of that time and the love her family shared filled her.

The flames around her grew stronger, given force by the emotion in her song. Roots that burst from the wet earth surrounding her, attempting to trap her, failed.

When you're feelin', lost alone in darkness
And you're needin', a friend to help you through this

I will find you, no matter where you're hidin'
I will find you, and I'll let you know that someone loves
I'll let the light in
Yeah, I'll let the light in

Alicia looked to the sky, raising her hands. She concentrated, maintaining her armor of fire, continuing to sing, and she called down a bolt of lightning. It struck the ground before her, but this bolt didn't disappear. It stayed there, vibrating, crackling, and shimmering.

Alicia stepped forward fearlessly into the light of the bolt, her hair rising and floating with the electricity. She was sucked up into the sky, speeding toward the clouds. She slowed to a stop before reaching the cloud cover. there she hovered above it all.

I'm flying! Ok, this is new, she thought. Alicia marveled at how she'd just done it. Like it was the most natural thing in the world. Instinctual. She giggled. *I didn't have standing on a lightning bolt on my bingo card, like, ever!* Alicia wondered what other magic had yet to be revealed, what witchy surprises might be in store.

Looking down into the valley below, she saw everything. Alicia could see Gran'Tree and his roots spread throughout. She could see Tawny fleeing toward the canyon pass, which was the entrance to this hellscape. She could see Madrigal, the earth giant, still bound tightly to the ground by the enormous roots.

The roots. It was all about the roots. Roots bring life and sustenance to the trees. It is their most vital part. Alicia recognized immediately that was where she needed to focus her energy, and she could not believe she had missed it before. But then she hadn't seen it all from this perspective, laid out so clearly before her.

Somewhere, A Legend Dies

Picking a target, Alicia summoned a new lightning bolt. She flew rapidly back to earth, traveling along the lines of electricity that vibrated down its length. The young witch landed next to one of the great roots holding Madrigal tight and let the bolt blink out of existence. Alicia stopped singing and spoke to the giant. "Be prepared."

"OH KAY."

She placed her fiery hands on the rough, swollen side of the root and sent her magic lancing across the surface. Huge flames erupted, igniting the bloody sap with a series of loud snapping, popping sounds. The magic burned the giant thing away.

"AAAAAAGGGHHH!! WHAAAT AAARE YOUUU DOII-ING?!?" Gran'Tree screamed in pain.

Alicia called down another burst of lightning, stepping into it and following it into the clouds. From this vantage point, she saw her next target and flew down on another bolt of electricity. She landed, stepped forward, and laid her hands upon a second root, burning it away in a brilliant, smoking blaze.

"NOOO, STOOOP! STOOOP THAAAT NOOOW!" the great tree bellowed.

Alicia repeated the process three more times, ignoring Gran'Tree's pleas. With the fifth root gone, Madrigal's arms were free, and he was able to sit up, his mountainous body rising into the air. He reached down with his long arms, and the earth giant tore at the last remaining roots covering his legs. Gran'Tree was in too much pain, trying to comprehend how this child could cause him so much damage, and didn't realize the giant was no longer bound.

Alicia flew into the clouds once again, studying the layout of roots below, seeing the network of lifelines and quickly devising

a plan. Gran'Tree didn't realize his greed had exposed him in this way, the swollen roots now too large to remain hidden underground. Alicia dove down to one side of the great tree and then the other, blasting flames into the roots from multiple sides, burning the tree's anchor cables.

Several roots rose into the air and snapped like whips. One connected with Alicia, knocking her from the bolt she rode. She fell like a blazing ball tracing a fiery line through the stormy sky.

Madrigal quickly stepped forward, reaching out with a giant hand, catching Alicia as she fell.

"Ugh, OOF!" The rough landing in his stony hand stole her breath for a moment. Scrambling to her feet, she ran to the edge of his palm. "Thanks!" she called back as a lightning bolt lanced from the sky ahead of her, and she leaped into the beam.

Back she flew into the sky, watching for the flailing roots now, strategically dodging and jumping to a new bolt when one of the whip-like things came too close. She was really getting the hang of this!

"Hooold stiiill!! Quiiit moooving youuu gnat!!" Gran'Tree wailed, whipping his branches around, flinging volley after volley of pine needles at the girl. But they all burned away before they could penetrate her armor. The fire magic was just too strong.

"Now, Mads, now!" she called to the earth giant. Once again, he lumbered forward, wrapping his arms around the great tree. But *this* time, the tree was weakened. It had lost many of its biggest roots, its anchors into the ground and the veins that channeled stolen blood to the tree. *This* time, Madrigal felt the tree wiggle in his grasp, like a loose tooth.

The giant continued to rock the tree from side to side, squeezing it tight, trying to get it to release its powerful grip on the earth. But Gran'Tree held firm, using all the strength he had gained from all the blood, from so many deaths. At the same time, the tree changed tactics with his branches and smashed them against Madrigal's head, repeatedly. He used the few roots swinging at Alicia to beat the sides and back of the earth giant, weakening Madrigal in the process.

Watching this unfold, Alicia rose into the clouds directly above Gran'Tree. From here, she could look down into the shattered crown of the tree and the huge split she had created. Alicia saw movement inside, quivering wet like a tumor, yellowish-red, and disgusting. Like gas from a swamp, the smell of corruption floated up into the air around her, almost choking her. Was this really the yellow pine's heart? Or maybe his brain? Either way, it didn't matter. She was ready to end this now. She needed to burn out the diseased thing.

Alicia began to hum the tune from the song again, a reminder of family, of campfires, smores, hot chocolate, and happiness. She held out her hands and gathered the power of the electricity that filled the clouds around her. At the same time, she reached inside herself and collected the magic of fire from within, condensing it, combining it with the electricity in her hands, creating a firestorm.

Alicia closed her eyes as the energies expanded around her. She thought about all the companions she had met on her adventures through the Wild Side. Mickey, Briar, Fiona, and Bristleback, true friends that helped her when she was lost. She thought about Elenos and Madrigal, creatures of such wonder as she could have never imagined. She thought about her birth parents, Thunderbolt and Vulcan, Ancients that came together to give her life. And then she thought about her *real* parents, the ones that had given her love

and taught her what it meant to care and be cared for her entire life. Her mom and dad, Kate and Richard.

Finally, she thought about Tawny, the wonderful cat she thought was dead, but who had come to save her when she needed it the most. Alicia opened her eyes and looked toward the mountain pass that led into the valley but did not see the cougar.

Good, she thought. She prayed that Tawny had found safety.

Holding the thoughts of these loved ones in her head, she called to the earth giant. "Stand back!" Madrigal released his hold on the great tree and took a step away. Gran'Tree immediately stopped his assault on the giant and turned his attention back toward the girl, his branches and roots rising to knock her from the sky once and for all.

Alicia looked back down into the dark depths of Gran'Tree's heart. She flexed her tingling fingers and pushed, sending the whirling firestorm plunging down through the rain, down past charred branches, down through the corrupted sap flowing from that wound like pus, down, down, down, and into the very center of the great yellow pine.

The response was instantaneous. The electricity paralyzed the tree, all its branches and roots standing out straight in all directions from the trunk, like a pufferfish that had been scared. Or a frightened porcupine.

The fire took hold there, in Gran'Tree's core, burning hotly in the wet mass as if it were filled with gasoline. Madrigal stepped forward between the extended roots, bent his craggy knees, and gripped the trunk of the huge tree tightly. He pulled hard with his arms while pushing up twice as hard with his stubby legs, his huge feet sinking deeply into the saturated earth.

The great tree lifted slowly and steadily. With a rumbling earthquake that was felt as far away as Thunderbolt's mountain, Madrigal tore the huge yellow pine from the earth, burned roots snapping and trailing behind it.

When he was sure the tree was fully freed from the ground, the earth giant spun like an Olympian and sent the trunk sailing through the air to the far side of the valley. Alicia's firestorm raged inside the great tree. Flames licked from within, emerging through cracks in the broken surface of the trunk. Huge gouts of fire exploded upward from the knotty eyes and great gash of a mouth, and carried in the sound of that inferno may have been a final, "Aaaahh . . ."

But Alicia couldn't be sure.

The magical fire ignored the rain that continued to fall gently. The storm was tapering off as the clouds started to break up and drift apart, sliding away over the peaks of the surrounding mountains. In no time at all, Gran'Tree was a huge blaze in the valley, becoming ash and charcoal, the reddish-brown sap draining and creating glistening sticky puddles that burned brightly.

Alicia used the last energy from the disappearing storm and zapped down to the earth. She watched the great tree, the heat from the fire warming her face and turning it pink. Slowly, Gran'Tree collapsed in on himself, burning from the inside, his vital fluids evaporating away, just as the victims of his deadly roots had collapsed. This was not vengeance. This was justice.

Justice had been served.

Alicia continued to watch until the flames died, and only then, allowed the fire still covering her to return to its source within.

She stepped closer to the earth giant and looked up into his green eyes. "You did good, Mads," she said.

"YOU DID GOOD TOO, ALIS," the giant responded, taking the first three letters of Alicia's name and adding a "z" sound to the end, like "alleys," just as she had done with his own name. He looked down at her and smiled a great, rocky smile as if he had gotten it right.

"Alis," Alicia said. "Well, my dad calls me Lish. But I accept. You can call me Alis."

"OH KAY. ALIS."

20

WHAT MATTERS THE MOST

Alicia found Tawny and Elenos waiting just beyond the mountain pass, and she hugged them tightly for a long time, feeling both the physical warmth of their bodies and the emotional warmth from within herself.

She climbed onto Elenos' back, and together the three turned north and headed toward the lake. The journey took a couple of days, but as before, she didn't mind. Alicia was simply happy. Truly, genuinely happy.

Madrigal had decided not to accompany them back. "I HAVE BEEN ASLEEP FOR SO LONG, AND EVERYTHING IS SO DIFFERENT AND NEW. I WANT TO SEE MORE OF THE WORLD. AND I WANT TO DISCOVER IF MY BROTHERS STILL LIVE."

"Just be careful, Mads," Alicia had told him. "Magic is new to the world of humankind. And if anyone sees you, they are going to be plenty scared, I can tell you that! Just wait for a bit. Stick to the wilderness. Maybe in time, humans will begin to understand and accept all this."

"I WILL, ALIS. IT WAS MY GREAT PLEASURE TO KNOW YOU."

"Same here, big guy. Same here. And I really hope we meet again someday. Until then, if you see any other beautiful lakes, try not to fall asleep there!" She laughed, and the great giant smiled and began to turn away but paused.

"ALIS, YOU ARE MORE THAN YOU BELIEVE YOU ARE. YOU MAY HAVE ACCOMPLISHED WHAT YOU WERE BORN TO DO, BUT YOU ARE SO MUCH MORE. KNOW THAT. GO AND LIVE YOUR LIFE. THE ADVENTURE IS FAR FROM OVER."

And with that, Madrigal turned and left, calling for his crew of birds to lead the way with their warnings.

That winter, it snowed heavily in Gran'Tree's valley, painting the valley and the surrounding mountains white with a thick blanket. The following summer, after the snow melted, there were two new lakes in the valley that had not been there before, both in the shape of giant feet.

Many years later, an explorer, having heard the tale of the great battle that occurred there and of the mighty warriors, Mads and Alis, went to investigate the valley himself to see the spot where it had all happened.

Entering the valley, he saw great furrows where the roots used to lay and the blackened remains of the huge tree crumbling into dust along the far edge. Wildflowers were beginning to return to the valley, and the explorer had never seen such a display of color. The perfumed scents drifting from the valley were almost overwhelming, and he was brought to tears at the beauty that lay before him.

He discovered the twin lakes and recalling the stories of the fight that had taken place there, he named one lake Mads Lake. The explorer had only heard the second warrior's name through stories told and retold for years. And as so often happens with these kinds of things, the story's details and the pronunciation of the name changed over time. So, he named the second lake Alice Lake.

Alicia finally returned home, riding up to the small cabin on the wondrous Elenos. She called loudly to her parents, "Mom! Dad!"

The front door flung open, and Kate and Richard, rushing from inside the small cabin, came to a sudden halt, their eyes wide and mouths agape.

"Yeah, that's pretty much the same expression I had when I first met him," Alicia said, laughing. "Mom? Dad? I'd like you to meet Elenos."

The moose knelt, and Alicia climbed down from his back and immediately ran to her parents, hugging them both fiercely. They remained huddled together for a long time, reluctantly pulling away and letting one another go.

Returning to the moose, who was once again standing, Alicia stroked his strong flank. "*It is time for me to go back to the wild, Alicia,*" Elenos told her. "*I am a solitary creature, not one to associate much with other species, especially humans.*"

"I understand," Alicia said. "And I appreciate the help you gave me. I know it was not an easy thing for you to do, to leave the hidden hills and to carry me to that valley. So, thank you. It was a once-in-a-lifetime pleasure that I will never forget."

Elenos sent an image of a female moose nuzzling her calf, and Alicia wondered once again if she was seeing the moose's own childhood. It was the same image he had sent once before, and she knew this meant the moose was showing care.

This image of nurturing brought to mind Alicia's interactions with Vulcan. The Ancient didn't think it was love, but Alicia was not so sure anymore. After all, there were a variety of ways to show it.

Alicia, smiling at the memory, gave the moose a final stroke along his forehead, stretching and touching the antlers one last time, then moved back as Elenos turned and slowly stepped away on his long legs, heading south.

Alicia learned later that Elenos had spoken to both her parents and told them of the adventure they had. He also sent them images of a fantastic battle and of the Burning Girl rising into the sky on a bolt of lightning.

Alicia returned to her parents. "I know the truth now," she said. "I know what I am, and I know who I am. But most important of all, I know I am your daughter because you have cared for me. I know you love me unconditionally. And that love is the strongest power of all. It's what matters the most. I love you both. And I have a lot to tell you."

And with that, she stepped forward once again into the arms of her parents and held them tightly. Tawny watched from a respectable distance, not wanting to disturb them.

There might have been a few tears.

THE END

AFTERWARD

Hi Readers!

And so ends The Moose Beach Trilogy. This unexpected series was born in June of 2018 at a small lake in the Boise National Forest. It started as a fairytale I wrote for my family to enjoy. A short story about a young girl who gets lost in the woods, discovers a magical realm, and needs to find her way home to her family. The story was inspired by my own experiences as a child, with summers spent at this very same lake, exploring these same woods. The Passage at Moose Beach was my first attempt at writing a book, and I was not prepared for the journey it would take me on.

Over the course of the next several years, the story grew. Fresh ideas for ways to expand Alicia and her world were coming to me, and at some point, I realized I was writing a sort of superhero origin story. That had never been my intention, but sometimes when writing, the story tells you where it wants to go and you just get dragged along for the ride.

Through edits, re-writes, major cuts, and lots and lots of encouragement and pushing from my publishers to get me to do things I didn't think I could, you now have the final product in your hands. Real world life events and the passing of loved ones have all influenced the direction of the story. But ultimately, it was the support of my family and friends who helped shape and drive this story to its conclusion.

I'd like to begin by thanking my wife Valeria, who first inspired me to write. Without her, this story wouldn't exist at all. And my

Afterward

daughter Sabrina, whose antics as a child helped me to understand and write from the perspective of a young girl. And to Jennifer, Kevin, Cori, Tom, Suzi, Steve, Tim, and the rest of my immediate friends who are as close as family and supported and encouraged this journey, you have my gratitude. To the early reader students of Robert Malone's 5th grade class at Rivera Elementary School, thank you for your early input (I'm glad you loved Bob the bear as much I do!) and for catching a critical continuity error in my first book! To my original publishers Marta and Kate of Z Girls Press, who fell in love with an early version of the story and pushed me beyond what I thought my limits were, thank you for not giving up. To my wonderful artist Gloria, who contributed purely for the love of the story, thank you for visualizing my characters. To my new partners, Ted, Clara, and Anna at Wisdom House Books, thank you for helping me get this final entry of the trilogy across the line and into the hands of my amazing readers.

And of course, to my parents Robert and Alice, whose souls will forever live in this story, thank you for everything.

I absolutely cannot end without thanking my extended friends/family of Warm Lake, Idaho. So, here's to Tawni, Ron, Sharon, and everyone else at North Shore Lodge who have treated me with such kindness and love that I feel their place is a home away from home. And to all the lovely cabin owners who have allowed my story to have a place in their homes, you all mean so much to me. There are simply too many to list (Bette, Rick, Jim, Brian, Krista, Scott, Frank, Nadine, Andrew, Fred, Ann, Stan, Ilmira, and on and on), you know who you are, and I appreciate you so much.

And finally, to all my readers, each and every one of you, thank you for spending your time with me in this world. Live, love, explore, be curious, ask why, seek answers, create, and be your best selves.

This is the end of this particular Wild Side story, but perhaps not the last time we'll visit this world. We will just have to see where the story tells me to go.

With my deepest thanks,
Michael Foster

ABOUT THE AUTHOR

Michael Foster lives in California and works full time in the video game industry. He is an avid gamer, musician, and reader. As a child, Michael spent long summers at his family's cabin in Idaho. He would endlessly explore the vast Boise National Forest around the cabin and lake, searching for hidden secrets tucked away in the shadowy spaces. Michael continues to spend as much time at his cabin as possible, and the Wild Side trilogy was imagined and written there. It has been an opportunity for Michael to rediscover his love of nature and the memories of childhood.

Michael has enjoyed watching his daughter grow into the same nature-loving and adventurous person he is, and draws writing inspiration from both his own experiences at the lake, and watching his family discover and enjoy the woods in their own way.

www.lakepointbooks.com
www.facebook.com/LakepointBooks/

www.ingramcontent.com/pod-product-compliance
Lightning Source LLC
LaVergne TN
LVHW061543070526
838199LV00077B/6887